the boy with the
lampshade
on his head

BRUCE WETTER

Atheneum Books for Young Readers
New York   London   Toronto   Sydney

This book is dedicated to all the children—both grown and
still growing—who feel left out, misplaced, or just plain
forgotten. Take the next step—a wonderful world awaits you.

ATHENEUM BOOKS FOR YOUNG READERS
An imprint of Simon & Schuster Children's Publishing Division
1230 Avenue of the Americas, New York, New York 10020

Book design by Ann Sullivan
The text for this book is set in Adobe Caslon.

Printed in the United States of America
First Edition
2 4 6 8 10 9 7 5 3 1

Library of Congress Cataloging-in-Publication Data
Wetter, Bruce.
The boy with the lampshade on his head / Bruce Wetter.
p. cm.
Summary: Shy fifth-grader Stanley Krakow spends his time trying
not to be noticed and pretending to be a superhero or
a record-breaking athlete, until one day he meets someone
who really needs him to be a hero.
ISBN 0-689-85032-8
[1. Bashfulness—Fiction. 2. Self-perception—Fiction. 3. Child
abuse—Fiction. 4. Schools—Fiction. 5. Family life—Fiction.]
I. Title. PZ7.W5329Bo 2004
[Fic]—dc21 2003004616

acknowledgments

Thanks first to my agent, Ashley Grayson, who took a chance on me. And to Caitlyn Dlouhy, my editor at Atheneum, who deserves much of the credit for this novel.
She has been unerring in her guidance.
Most of all, I would like to thank my wife, Mari-Ann.
She is a light shining in the darkness, and an inspiration to become the person God intended me to be.

1

uncle willie's hideout

It didn't matter when Stanley got home from school, he always walked in at exactly the wrong time. It was a talent he had. Not a secret identity talent, like when he pitched for the Dodgers or set records on ESPN. But a talent nonetheless. And one thing Stanley had learned in his short life was this: Talent could not be hidden. He knew, because he had tried. About a month after fifth grade had begun, when Stanley had first noticed his amazing but unwanted talent, he'd experimented with coming home a little later than planned. For a few weeks after that he'd experimented with hurrying home early. He even experimented with coming home just when he was supposed to, which no one could have possibly expected. None of it did any good. The wrong time seemed to lurk just behind his front door, waiting for him.

Sure enough, even though on this particular afternoon Stanley had stood for nearly two whole minutes with his USA Hospital Association–certified stethoscope pressed against the front door, listening for enemy activity, it wasn't until his hand actually turned the doorknob and pushed that his mom's voice blasted through the room. "You!" she began, shouting at Stanley's older brother, Jerry. "Outside!" Jerry looked away from the basketball spinning on his finger just long enough for it to wobble and fall. "That, young man, is exactly why you should have been outside in the first place. And you!" she added, turning to Stanley, her radar eyes pinning his feet motionless even before he'd made it past the WELCOME TO OUR WONDERFUL HOME mat. "Go play with your friends or go to the library, but stay out of the house! I have a million things to do!"

"News flash, Mom," Jerry tossed back. "Ever think that we live here too? Ever think that maybe we'd like to be the ones having the party tonight and order *you* out?"

Stanley dropped his book bag, sweatshirt, and lunch box as he hurried across the living room, hoping he could reach the back door before the yelling got too loud. "Jerry," he heard his mom say, her voice rising with each word, "I don't want any arguments. Not today. I'm nervous enough as is. Understand? This is the first party I've had since . . . since . . ." She seemed to lose focus, like a kite with its string cut.

"Since the last one," Stanley said, trying to be helpful. He didn't add that at the last party Uncle Willie had locked himself in the bathroom and they'd had to call the police and an ambulance and break the door down.

"Butt kisser," Jerry sneered at his brother. Then, to his mom, "Fine, I'm leaving anyway. I'll be at Alvin's, not that anyone gives a—"

"Watch your mouth!" their mom warned.

Whatever Jerry said was drowned out by the noise of him slamming out the front door. Stanley quietly slipped out the back, then hurried for his hideout under the house.

The hideout had been Uncle Willie's idea. The only the thing was, Uncle Willie hadn't seen it yet, on account of after three months they still hadn't let him out of the hospital. Or maybe Uncle Willie didn't want to come out of the hospital—Stanley was never quite sure about that part. Either way, the hideout had already saved Stanley's life close to a gazillion times. He wiggled the screen free and scooted through a two-foot gap in the concrete foundation, then felt around in the dark for the extension cords, plugging them together when he found them. Strings of Christmas lights went on everywhere. That had been Uncle Willie's idea too.

"Let's get out of here, take a walk, just us two," Uncle Willie had said just before the last party, the one where the police and ambulance had come. Uncle Willie liked to take walks, especially before parties. During them too. "Too many people," he told Stanley, looking whiter and pastier than he usually did, which was pretty white and pasty. "Vaporizes the part of my brain that controls my mouth. It's not that I can't think of what to say—actually, I have so much pounding around in my head that I can't get it out! I think of one thing, then I think of another, and by the time I come up with what to say, the conversation's moved on. Know what I mean, Stanley, my man?"

Stanley nodded; he knew exactly what his uncle meant. Hardly any of the other kids even talked to him anymore, on account of whenever someone asked him something, it took Stanley so long to think of an answer that by the time he was ready, no one was listening. You just couldn't be too careful when answering a question—that was Stanley's philosophy. After all, there were millions and millions of wrong answers and only one right one. Get one answer wrong, get even one *word* wrong, and the entire class might start laughing. Just thinking about it, Stanley felt his hands start shaking and his face turning red with shame. Given a choice between saying nothing and being laughed at, Stanley would choose silence every time.

Uncle Willie had given Stanley a pat on the shoulder as they walked. "You're a good listener," his uncle said. "And being a good listener is most of what being a good conversationalist is about." That was another thing Stanley liked about Uncle Willie—you could say the right thing without saying a word. "Not that anyone at one of your mom's parties would ever know that," Uncle Willie said with a sigh. They had circled the block and were now walking ever more slowly in the direction of Stanley's house. "I don't know why your mom makes me come to these things. She knows I don't fit in. You know how it feels, smiling at people, trying to think of the right thing to say, while they're looking at you like you're some kind of lampshade? Waiting for the light to go on and secretly thinking that the bulb probably needs changing?"

Everyone was always saying how much alike he

and Uncle Willie were, but even so, Stanley was surprised that his uncle would know about lampshades. "Uncle Willie," he started, wanting to ask his uncle if he had ever played the lampshade game. But his uncle motioned for silence.

"Move slowly," Uncle Willie whispered, pointing at Stanley's house, at the spot where Stanley's mom stood on the front porch, hands on her hips, tapping her foot the same way she did when the principal called to say Stanley had gotten in trouble at school again. "They only strike when they sense fear." He laughed at his joke, but the sound that came out sounded more like gargling. "Oh well, time to face the music," he said. "I don't suppose you have a convenient hideout located nearby?" he asked. "Somewhere I could comfortably change into my superhero outfit?"

Stanley's mouth dropped open, but before he could say anything, his mom started: "I swear, Willie, you'll be late for your own funeral! I invite a date for you, and what do you do? Disappear!"

"I wish," Uncle Willie muttered under his breath, nudging Stanley. Only Stanley was still thinking about what his uncle had said—was he serious? Was this his uncle's way of telling him that he, too, had a secret identity? Stanley stared at his uncle as they climbed the porch steps, at the thick glasses, crooked smile, and thinning hair, even though he was ten years younger than his sister, Stanley's mom. Who would ever suspect? And all those trips he took for his company? Maybe the reason Uncle Willie didn't talk about them wasn't because they were boring, like Uncle Willie was always saying they were; maybe it was because when you had a secret identity, you couldn't tell anyone about all the amazing adventures you had—one of the biggest drawbacks to being secretly famous, as Stanley knew so well.

"A hideout," Uncle Willie hissed as Stanley's mom took his arm, steering him through the door and toward a young woman. He looked over his shoulder at Stanley on the porch. "By the next party. Without fail!"

the famous stanley krakow

Besides the Christmas lights, Stanley had outfitted the hideout with pieces of carpet that the neighbors had thrown away, so he didn't have to sit in the dirt. The carpet pieces smelled strongly of cats, which was exactly why Stanley had chosen them: The smell was sure to confuse any mutant underground dirt dwellers in search of a quick human meal. He'd also stocked the place with candles and a flashlight in case the electricity ever went out, little pull-the-tab cans of ant-proof tuna, and the entire set of *Encyclopædia Britannica* that his dad had bought for him and Jerry, only nobody seemed to notice it wasn't in their room anymore. Stanley had read almost a third of the volumes already. By the end of fifth grade he figured he'd be through the entire set. That just had to be a record, Stanley thought—maybe not an ESPN-type of record, though. More like a *Guinness Book of World Records* record. Stanley sucked his upper lip into his mouth, biting at it, trying to remember if he'd ever been on the *Guinness World Records* show. Of course, they would have to let him wear his Famous Stanley Krakow disguise, which is what ESPN always did. If the kids at school ever discovered how famous he was, they would bother him for autographs all the time, and he wouldn't be able to concentrate on his schoolwork, which his mom told him at least a hundred times a week was the most important thing in the world.

Stanley's hideout was just beneath all the heating and cooling pipes, and by pressing his stethoscope against them, he could listen in on conversations throughout the house. He'd even labeled the pipes, to tell what room he was spying on. Today, though, all he could hear were the sounds of his mom cooking in the kitchen, and after a few minutes even that stopped. Stanley picked up the *Encyclopædia Britannica*, volume eight, *Edward to Extract*, opened to his bookmark, and concentrated. Rules were rules, after all, and the rules clearly stated that he must understand every word of what he was reading.

It wasn't until a few articles later that Stanley smelled the smoke from the kitchen. He was just wondering if he should go inside and let his mom know that her dinner was burning when he heard her shriek. Then he heard her shriek again. One shriek might mean she needed help, but two shrieks was a definite 'stay away' signal. Still, he listened carefully, on account of wasn't his mom always telling him how a good vocabulary made all the difference in life? Even his brother, Jerry, was surprised at some of the words Stanley had picked up through the heating vents. "Whoa!" Jerry had said the last time he'd looked through the little pocket notebook Stanley kept for just this purpose. "Now, there's a word that could come in handy! And you're telling me mom actually said that? You know, she might be sharper than I thought."

Unfortunately, all he could hear after his mom opened the kitchen windows was some muttering and the twang of pots and pans whacking into the sink. He didn't even hear the sound of fire engines, which meant that it couldn't have been much worse than a minor catastrophe. Probably, he and Jerry would be eating whatever she'd burned for lunch tomorrow.

Stanley had just pulled volume eight back on his

lap when he heard a vehicle pull into the driveway, and then a knock on the kitchen door. He immediately crawled to the kitchen heating pipe, donning his stethoscope. "Julie's delivery," a man said—Julie's was a fancy restaurant that his mom and dad never took him to. Then he heard the sound of the door opening. "Ten salads à la Julie," he heard the man say. "Ten veal parmigianas with scalloped potatoes and creamed peas. Two loaves of garlic bread. Two carrot cakes. *Bon appétit*, Mrs. Krakow."

"Stanley," his mom said very quietly after the man had left—Stanley could tell she was talking right into the heating vent—"bring one of the garbage cans into the kitchen." Before he could even think of pretending that he couldn't hear her, his mom added, "And don't even think of pretending that you can't hear me. Especially with your new stethoscope."

When he came into the kitchen, dragging the garbage can behind him, his mom was busy scooping the food out of the restaurant boxes it had come in and into the glass dishes that she used for cooking. "But isn't it already cooked?" Stanley asked.

"Out!" his mom yelled. And she didn't even thank him for the garbage can.

The problem was that he was bored with his book, and his friend Robby couldn't play, and his bottom was getting sore from sitting under the house for so long. So when he heard the shower running in his parents' bathroom, he crept back into the house, quietly moving into the living room. Without a sound, he slid toward the big floor lamp standing behind his dad's reading chair, then carefully removed the lampshade, shifting the lamp behind the nearby window curtains and placing the lampshade on his head. It was time for the lampshade game.

Stanley loved hiding games of all kinds, probably because he was such a genius at disappearing. If the game was to hide, then not only could he be a hero—he held the all-time ESPN hide-and-seek record—but there wasn't a chance in the world that anyone would laugh at him. How could they, if they couldn't find him? It was perfect! Well, almost perfect. Stanley couldn't help but remember the time when he'd set the ESPN record: five hours and ten minutes. They never did actually find him; he'd only given up when his mom and dad began hollering all over the neighborhood that if he didn't come out instantly, he'd be on restriction until the day after he died. Only he couldn't quite squeeze out of the tree hole that he'd squeezed into. Had the tree shrunk in the hours he'd been sitting there? Or could it be that it was tree dinnertime, with him as the munchy-crunchy tree meal? That was when

Stanley had begun screaming, and by the time the fire-men had finally pulled him out, half the neighborhood was gathered around, clapping and cheering. The other half was watching the rescue on TV.

All in all, under the lampshade behind his dad's chair was a far safer place to hide. The shade was made from a frilly web of strings that covered him almost to his waist, while the rest of him was mostly hidden by his dad's chair. Stanley could see through the lamp-shade easily enough, but turning his head always caused the lacy strings to bounce. Also, he sometimes had to sneeze from all the dust.

The only drawback to the lampshade game was that ESPN refused to televise it. Stanley didn't really blame them—after all, he was the only one who even knew it was a game. On the other hand, every record he set was a world record. First record—how many times his mom and dad walked past without noticing him: twenty. Second record—how many minutes he stood there before being discovered: fifty-two. There was actually a third record, only it was difficult to measure—how loud they yelled when they finally found him. Stanley had thought of buying a sound gauge, like one he had seen displayed in the electron-ics store next to his dad's grocery store, only he didn't think his parents would appreciate that type of input.

Today, staring through the thin fabric of the lamp-shade, he counted his mom passing by twenty-one times before his dad even got home. Of course, she was nervous about the party, so Stanley didn't feel quite as victorious as he usually did when he broke a record. Actually, he felt sort of guilty, watching his mom set a bowl of nuts on one table, then move it to another table, then back again, over and over and over. She looked as though she was going to cry.

When his dad came in from work, he immediately went to his reading chair and opened the newspaper. Stanley held his breath—his dad had never sat there during the lampshade game before. "You're late," his mom said to him. "You'd better get ready for the party. And don't eat any of those nuts!" she said as he reached for the bowl.

"I'll get ready in a minute, dear," he said, flipping through the pages of the paper. "Just a bit of relaxation to take the edge off, that's all I need." His dad watched as his mom stomped back into the kitchen. "Probably burned the food again," he muttered to himself. Then he sniffed the air. "Julie's," he finally said. "This din-ner'll cost me a fortune." He sighed. "Well . . . let's see who had a worse day than I did." Through the lamp-shade, Stanley watched his dad shuffle the pages until he reached the obituary section. "Do you believe it?" he said to himself. "Look at who died—old man Morrison!" He chuckled. "Now, that's what I consider a worse day than mine." Stanley smiled too. It was almost as if he and his dad were reading the paper together. Stanley leaned closer to the chair, waiting for his dad to notice him.

Just then Jerry opened the front door, hurrying in. "Hey, dweeb," he said to Stanley as he passed. "How long you going to wear the lampshade? And Mom wonders why I never invite any friends over." Stanley said nothing, of course. It would have been against the rules. "Hey, butt brain! I'm talking to you! Geez, Dad, do I have to live with this geek?"

"Quiet!" his dad shouted. "A little quiet, is that too much to ask? It's been a heck of a day, okay?" He snapped the paper down, staring behind the chair. "Jerry, put the lampshade back on the lamp where it belongs and get your backside to the dinner table! No wonder it's always so dark in here."

Jerry rolled his eyes. "That's Stanley, Dad. I'm Jerry. Remember? I came first, he came second?"

His dad's face turned the color of a beet, fingers knotting into the paper. "You, buddy boy," he said to Jerry, "are cruising for a bruising! Now into the kitchen! Both of you!"

Stanley put the lampshade back on the lamp, then

walked off toward the kitchen, staring at his watch. "Another record," he muttered with a sigh. One hour two minutes. He wondered what the record was for his dad talking to him. Shorter than that, he figured. A lot shorter.

stanley's secret assignment

After he and his brother had eaten, Stanley had no choice but to go outside, on account of Jerry was doing homework in their room and said if Stanley even made a sound, he would tie him up, gag him, and hang him from a hook in the closet. "Don't play in here!" his mom had said when Stanley came into the living room. "Everything is clean, and I want it to stay that way!"

"So why have a party?" Stanley asked.

"Out! It'll be light for another hour. Go play with your friends!"

Stanley closed the front door behind him and wandered toward the sidewalk, wondering which friends his mom could possibly be talking about. Well, there was Robby Lanorsky, of course, but Robby almost *had* to be his friend, on account of he lived right across the street. Anyway, Stanley had better things to do than count up all the kids in the neighborhood who weren't his friends; at the moment he was deeply involved in trying to time and categorize the various rumblings coming from his stomach. He'd been wrong about having the burned meal for lunch tomorrow—they'd had it for dinner.

"Interesting," Jerry had said at the kitchen table, pushing the food around on his plate. "This is what you're feeding your guests? Who's coming to the party, anyway, Smokey the Bear?"

"Very funny," his mom had answered. "Just eat your dinner. It's perfectly good food. I scraped all the burned parts off, so no complaining."

"Who's complaining?" Jerry had said, winking at Stanley. "I mean, just today in science class we studied how important carbon is to human life. So, Mom, I don't think of this as burned, I think of it as carbon rich." He took a bite, made a face. "Mmm, and so much tastier than charcoal."

"Just eat the dinner!" his mom had yelled. Jerry and

Stanley had kept their heads down, trying to stifle their laughter. "Comedians," their mom had muttered. "Other mothers get kids, I get comedians."

"Hey, Stan!" Robby hollered from his bedroom window as Stanley wandered past, still listening to his stomach rumble. He had clearly identified three quite distinct rumblings, which corresponded to the three lumps of food his mom had served them—though, to be completely honest, he wasn't exactly sure what they had eaten. One burned dish, after all, looked pretty much the same as the next.

Robby hollered again, hammering the windowsill with one of his tennis shoes. "Earth to Stan, Earth to Stan!" he shouted. "Please connect your life-support system!"

Stanley turned and saw Robby's grinning face pressed up against the screen of his bedroom window, nose flattened. He immediately glanced up and down the street, checking for spies; there were only a couple of kids a block away, playing basketball. Still, he felt his face blushing. "Hi," he said, barely loud enough to hear.

Robby laughed. "Man, Stan, I bet you were thinking again. I never saw anyone who can think so hard— I mean, you about walked right past! I guess that's what it takes to be the smartest kid in the neighborhood, huh?"

Stanley didn't know if Robby was kidding him or not. Anyway, Amy Fitzwaters was way smarter than he was—but did she live in the neighborhood? Stanley wasn't exactly certain. He kicked at the ground, his face turning from pink to watermelon red. One thing was for sure: No one spying on him would ever suspect that the Stanley Krakow who lived on Lamont Drive across from Robby Lanorsky was actually the Very Famous Stanley Krakow who held so many records and pitched for the Dodgers and gave such great interviews on ESPN almost every week. When the Stanley Krakow who lived across from Robby Lanorsky had to say something, he usually turned white and his hands shook and it was hard for him to breathe. At least this time, instead of turning white, he was turning red.

"Stan, you okay?" Robby said from his window. "Try breathing. It works pretty well for the rest of the world's population. Hey, listen, Stan—I can't come out 'cause I have to do my homework, and you can't come in and help me 'cause tomorrow my dad's going to drive me and George and Jimmy to the lake, and my mom says I have to do my homework myself if I want to go. You ever catch crawdads, Stan? George says he'll teach us. Want to come?"

Stanley shook his head. His stomach began rumbling again, adding several urgent new tones to the variation—just the thought of spending the day with George and Jimmy upset him. Robby might have to be his friend, on account of living right across the street, but George and Jimmy lived all the way on the next block. Then he remembered that his mom was always telling him how it was impolite to answer without words. "No," he managed to say.

"No?" Robby said. "What do you mean, no? No, you can't come with us, or no, you never caught crawdads? Either way, Stan, you have to come. A definite must-do type of thing." Robby lowered his voice, cupping his hands around his mouth. "I mean, George is a nice guy and everything, but . . . you're the one who knows everything, right? You're the one who has all the answers. I'm right, aren't I? Well, aren't I?" Stanley looked up, grinning shyly. "Yes!" Robby shouted. "Stanley the Brain is coming with us! Yes! We will catch a gazillion crawdads! Yes! We will be the heroes of the known world!"

Somewhere in the house Stanley heard Robby's mom asking him if he was doing his homework. At the same time a large moving van rumbled onto their street, heading in their direction. They both turned to stare at it. The last time someone had moved into the neighborhood had been . . . Stanley couldn't even remember how long it'd been. "Robert," Mrs. Lanorsky called, "you had better be at your desk and not at the window." As the van came toward them Stanley could see a large, unsmiling man behind the steering wheel and a large, unsmiling woman next to him. Squished against the passenger's side door, a skinny, dark-eyed girl stared out the window. As the van passed she smiled and waved. Stanley realized his mouth was hanging open. He shut it so hard, his teeth rattled. Then he remembered to wave back. The van was already halfway down the next block.

"Smooth," Robby told his friend. "Very . . . casual. You need some work on your timing, though."

"Robert Henry," Robby's mother warned, her voice nearer this time, "you had better not be talking to Stanley. Stanley's outside and you're inside because he already has good grades!"

"Exactly why you might want to consider letting him come in," Robby yelled over his shoulder.

"Robert!"

"Okay, okay! I'm doing my homework, already!" Robby turned back to the window. "We'll pick you up at noon," he hissed. "Be ready when you hear the secret honk." He disappeared into his room, then reappeared almost immediately. "Find out who the new people are. That's your assignment. Whose house are they moving into? What do they have in the van? Guns? Coffins? Illegal aliens? And don't get caught!" he warned. "They could be spies! Criminals! Even alien pod people!"

4

crawdads

On the way to the lake the next morning Robby and George got to sit in the front with Mr. Lanorsky. That was all right with Stanley, on account of he was afraid that Robby might ask him how the spying had gone, and he'd have to say that he hadn't really found anything out, on account of the new people had moved into the old McKersky house, the one totally surrounded by a wall of shrubs. Stanley had wanted to crawl into the shrubs to spy, but then he thought maybe the new people had a watchdog. He couldn't actually hear a watchdog, but he figured any watchdog worth his weight wouldn't make a sound until just after it had bit someone's leg in two. Try explaining that to his mom!

Stanley had to sit in the back with Jimmy Jones, who moved as far away from Stanley as he could, staring out the window. Not that Stanley minded—whenever Jimmy talked to him, he never knew what to say anyway. "Loser," Jimmy would sneer when Stanley didn't answer. "Total, wimpoid loser."

Mr. Lanorsky, on the other hand, talked to Stanley all the time, and not even once ever seemed to notice that Stanley wasn't talking back. In fact, when Mr. Lanorsky talked, it was like Stanley and he were having a great conversation. "Hey, Stanley," he said, shifting the rearview mirror so that Stanley could see that he was smiling, "you grow any hair on your chest yet? You know, you can't be a man until you grow hair on your chest. Well?" Stanley just grinned and shook his head. "Not even one little hair? I bet you George has some hair on his chest. George comes from a very hairy family."

"We do too!" Robby shouted. He climbed over George and began unbuttoning Mr. Lanorsky's shirt, which was what he always did when his dad mentioned hairy families. "Look at that mop!" He smiled, pulling his father's shirt open.

"Ow!" Mr. Lanorsky said as Robby yanked out a hair, only they all knew he was only playing. "All right, son, glue that on to Stanley's chest. How's he going to catch crawdads without hair on his chest?" Stanley laughed as Robby flipped into the backseat.

"Morons!" Jimmy muttered, staring out the window.

Sometimes, when Stanley was alone with Robby and his dad, Mr. Lanorsky would say, "Stanley, it's not your fault. It's genetic. You just come from an unhairy family. When's your dad going to grow some hair on his chest? Huh? He probably just needs a good swig of hair tonic."

"Apes come from hairy families," Stanley always answered. "My dad's smart; he doesn't need hair."

Talking to Mr. Lanorsky was so easy and natural that Stanley didn't even notice he was doing it. Not when they were alone, at least. It was totally impossible to even imagine Mr. Lanorsky ever laughing or making fun of him. Besides, Mr. Lanorsky always acted like it was the most normal thing in the world for Stanley to talk. Usually, Stanley never had time to think about it, because that was when Mr. Lanorsky would start to make ape noises. Then he would grab Robby and Stanley, tickling them until they couldn't stand up. "Ugh, ugh," Mr. Lanorsky would grunt, laughing.

"Pretty good for a hairy, ignorant ape, huh?"

Actually, Stanley didn't know whether his dad's chest was hairy or not, since his dad was usually dressed and off to work before everyone else got up. Even on Saturdays and Sundays. Stanley's mom always told Jerry and Stanley not to bother their dad in the morning, on account of his coffee hadn't started working yet and he was grumpy. The problem was, he wasn't any less grumpy when he got home at night. Stanley figured his coffee must have worn off by then.

Once Stanley had asked his dad why he couldn't take them places on Saturdays and Sundays like Mr. Lanorsky did. "Because I'm a boss," his dad had said. "If the boss isn't at work, nothing gets done. Always remember that, boys: Your dad's a boss. And besides, it costs too much to hire someone else. You know how much money it takes to raise you?"

"A damn lot?" Jerry said, trying not to smile. Their dad said the same thing to them almost every time.

"Wiseass," their dad muttered. "Damn straight it costs a lot!"

Mr. Lanorsky dropped them off at the part of the lake where the cliff came down almost to the shore. There wasn't any beach, only places where the water had worn away the cliff, making small inlets. Robby, Jimmy, and George ran down to the water. Stanley walked. He'd been there before and remembered that the water was actually just a thick, oozy muck. What if it came alive? Stanley glanced to the right and to the left—not a single kid in sight. Maybe there was a reason nobody caught crawdads. Maybe it was the crawdads that were doing the catching.

"Hey, superwimp!" Jimmy cried to Stanley. "You going to join us or not?"

"Okay," Robby said, "let's get some crawdads!" Everyone had a plastic bucket; Robby was already taking off his shoes. "So what do we do?" he asked George.

"My brother told me it's easy. Just find a crawdad and scoop him up! He said they're too stupid even to swim away."

Robby stared into the water and frowned. "Sure," he said. "But what's a crawdad look like?"

George didn't answer right away. He got his bucket and stepped onto a rock, looking into the water. Robby and Jimmy moved just behind him, staring where he stared. Finally, he said, "I don't exactly know. I mean, not absolutely exactly. I thought a crawdad would look, well, you know . . . like a crawdad."

"Aww!" Jimmy moaned. "What a dip!"

Robby turned to where Stanley was standing several feet back. "Hey, Stan! I bet you know what a crawdad looks like, don't you? Stan knows practically every-thing," he explained to the others. "Right, Stan?"

Stanley nodded and did his best to smile. He was suddenly very glad that he had gone under the house to read the *Encyclopædia Britannica* instead of watch-ing Saturday-morning cartoons. It had taken a while, but he'd finally figured it out. Crawdads were actually crayfish, only the ones they were looking for weren't even crayfish, they just looked like them.

"Well?" Jimmy said, staring at Stanley. "What's the story? And you'd better have it too! Otherwise, maybe we'll use you for bait. Crawdad bait!"

"They're, uh . . . they're . . ." Stanley felt the blood drain out of his face. His hands started to tremble.

"Not that again!" Jimmy said. "Aww, we should've brought our fishing poles."

"Don't let Jimmy bother you." Robby winked. "He can't catch fish, either." Then Robby smiled and whis-pered, "Just point to one. Okay?"

Stanley took a deep breath and walked over to the rock George was standing on. He figured any muck monster would have grabbed George by then, so it was probably safe. Of course, a muck monster might have decided that George didn't look very tasty, on account of he was sort of too skinny and too tall. Slowly, care-fully, Stanley bent toward the water, staring downward, hoping that whatever he saw would look like the picture in the encyclopedia. Only what it looked like was muck, and not just any muck, but the type of muck that reminded him of the slimy space aliens on the late-night movies that he was never supposed to watch when his mom and dad went out. It also looked a lot like the burned dinner his mom had forced them to eat the night before. His stomach began to rumble. Stanley wondered what his friends would do if he threw up on the crawdads. If they really were crawdads, that was, and not aliens. If he threw up on aliens, they just might be in serious trouble.

That was when he saw it. A crawdad, just like it looked in the encyclopedia, resting right on top of a mucky, space alien rock. "There!" Stanley shouted. "There's one!"

Robby ran over. "Where? Where?" So Stanley showed him. "Wow!" he shouted. "A real live crawdad! Zamborific!" That was the word Robby always used whenever something was as cool and perfect as it was on the lost world of Zambor.

"Scoop it up!" Jimmy said.

"You scoop it up!" Robby shot back. "We found it!"

So Jimmy stepped onto the rock, which wasn't all that big. "Where?" he asked, and Robby pointed to it. "Do they bite? They look like they might bite.

Anyway, George's the expert; let's let him scoop it up."

"Yeah," Robby agreed. "George's the expert, let him scoop it up!" So George balanced on the rock carefully as Jimmy and Robby pointed again at the crawdad. Only instead of scooping it up, George slipped and fell in the lake.

For a minute no one said a thing. Then George finally stood up, covered with muck. "Oh, gross!" Robby frowned. "You are definitely not riding home in the front seat!"

"So where's he going to sit?" Jimmy sneered. "Not in the back, that's for sure!"

"In the trunk!" Robby and Jimmy announced at the same moment, smiling and slapping high fives. That got everyone laughing, even George. He climbed back onto the rock, and everyone laughed even harder on account of there was this green gunk hanging all over him. He looked like one of those trees in *The Land Before Time* or something.

That was when George started jiggling all around and pulling at his pants. "I think I caught a crawdad!" he yelled. "I think I really did!"

the adventures of dark man

"We caught five crawdads!" Stanley shouted as he ran into his house.

"You're late and you're filthy," his mom said. "Straight into the bathroom with you, young man." But before he got halfway there, she shouted, "Wait!" and walked toward him. "You don't have one of those creatures in your pocket, do you? I don't want to find another one in the bathtub."

"Mom, that was Jerry." She continued staring at him, her X-ray eyes taking him apart, bone by bone. "And it wasn't a crawdad, Mom, it was a lizard." Still, his mom didn't look away. "Okay, okay," he finally said. "I don't have a crawdad in my pocket." He didn't add that it was in the mop bucket in the garage. His mom never mopped on weekends. Not usually, at least.

When Stanley came out of the bathroom, his mom was already in her "going out" dress, which meant that Jerry would be fixing his famous egg-and-bologna-cup sandwiches for dinner. His mom never cooked when she was going out because she said that it might ruin her good looks. Which was just fine with Stanley—he loved bologna-cup sandwiches, especially since nobody else even knew what they were.

First, Jerry toasted some bread, then he fried a couple of eggs. Last, he tossed a few slices of bologna into the pan. In about twenty seconds the bologna curled up into a cup, and Jerry shouted, "Ready!" The eggs went into the bologna cups, and the bologna went onto a slice of toast. They had to eat the whole thing before the bologna got flat. Also, they had to eat the entire egg yolk in one bite, so that it didn't drip. Those were the rules. In just eighteen minutes they ate ten sandwiches, practically a record. Then their mom came in and yelled at them because of the mess they'd made. "You two had better clean this all up before your dad and I get back tonight!" she told them as she walked toward the front door. Cleaning up a mess ruined her good looks even more than cooking. Their dad followed just behind her, shaking his head.

Jerry ran to their room the moment the front door closed, flipping the lights off and peeking out the shutters to make sure his parents were really leaving. He watched them get into his mom's car and drive off, then waited a few minutes to make sure they hadn't forgotten anything. Then he began getting ready to go out too.

"You promised you'd stay!" Stanley yelled as Jerry slid out of his T-shirt. "You told Mom and Dad you wouldn't sneak out! You said you'd take good care of me!"

Jerry didn't even pause. He slid out of his dirty pants and into a clean pair. "I lied," he said with a smirk. He rubbed under each arm with a washrag, then grabbed a stick of deodorant, caking his armpits.

"But I don't like to be alone! I'll be your slave, I'll do anything you want!" Stanley begged.

Jerry flipped the key to his dad's car that he'd stolen into the air. "If you were really my brother," he said, the key flopping back into his hand, "and not some mutant, adopted, jellyfish alien, you'd come with me."

But Stanley already knew about going out with Jerry. That was even worse than staying at home. The last time Jerry and his friend Alvin Bagley stole their dad's car, Alvin had a bottle of liquor, and they drove all around the park, whistling at girls and trying to get them to climb in with them. The amazing part was that two girls actually did! Stanley couldn't believe it! He sure wouldn't have gotten in the car with Jerry and Alvin. They weren't even old enough to drive! Only he was already in the car, so he didn't have much of a choice.

Not only that, but when they got to a dark part of the park, Jerry had made Stanley get out and walk around, watching for police—as if Stanley had really wanted to stay and watch them kissing! Then Jerry and Alvin started getting sick on account of the liquor, so the girls left, calling them a bunch of toads. Not Stanley, of course—they told Stanley that he was cute and that he should call them up sometime. For a while Jerry drove around looking for them, but people kept honking and yelling for him to get off the road. One man even tried to force Jerry to stop the car, only Jerry just gave him the finger and told him—well, Stanley wasn't allowed to say words like that, but the other guy said he was going to call the police. After that Jerry had to park along the curb every time car lights came by, and they all had to lie on the floor. Lying on the floor of a car with two guys who're getting sick every five minutes was not Stanley's idea of fun.

So there was nothing for Stanley to do but listen to Jerry drive off in their dad's car. As soon as the car noise faded, Stanley ran to all the windows and doors, locking every one of them. Then he turned off the TV, because how was he going to hear if someone was breaking in if the TV was on? That's what worried him most—people breaking in. And monsters, of course; he worried about monsters quite a lot. And werewolves, especially on full-moon nights. Stanley always tried to keep his parents home on full-moon nights, but they never quite seemed to grasp the situation. Then there were zombies, alien intruders, vampires . . .

"Aaaah!" Stanley yelled. He ran to his dresser, pawing through his socks and underwear until he found his black hooded mask. Then he ran into his parents' room. Stanley Krakow, Man of Action! He dug through his dad's desk, pulling out what looked like a piece of bamboo until you pressed a secret button, and then it became a supersharp killer weapon—his dad's special knife, the one he said came from "the war." His dad had told him that if he ever, ever touched it, it would be the end of him forever. Only it wasn't Stanley who touched it, because Stanley had already put on his black hood, which magically turned him into Dark Man. And it was perfectly all right for Dark Man to use the knife. Dark Man was even more powerful and famous than the Famous Stanley Krakow, and nobody, not zombies or werewolves or even alien intruders, would have the guts to sneak into a house guarded by Dark Man. Or so he hoped.

After Jerry left, Dark Man crawled from room to room, invisible to all, waiting for any sign of attack. Nothing could touch Dark Man, nothing could pierce his dark veil, nothing could withstand his terrible knife, Slash! Fearless and bold, Dark Man slid open Stanley's closet doors, jabbing inside. "Hah!" he shouted with each thrust. "Come out, come out, creatures of the night! I dare you!" He lifted up his bedspread, peeking under the bed. Nothing. "Afraid?" he shouted. "You should be!" Dark Man waved his knife through the inky blackness, watching huge dust balls scatter at his touch. He would have to talk to the wench who cleaned the place about doing a better job. "Hah!" he shouted again, then moved on to the hall closet.

There was only one small problem with Dark Man: He lost all his power upon falling asleep, which was why Stanley always hid inside the laundry hamper at the first sign of drowsiness. The laundry hamper, he had discovered, was the one place in the entire house that was totally invulnerable to attack. In fact, the laundry hamper might be the one place in the entire universe that was totally invulnerable to attack. It was

the socks, of course. Jerry's gym socks. The smell radi-
ated outward, creating the perfect cloaking device, a
force so powerful that nothing yet discovered by mod-
ern scientists—either human or alien—could pene-
trate.

Take the night Uncle Willie had locked himself in
the bathroom, for instance. Even after they'd broken
down the door, even after his mom and his dad and the
police and the ambulance people had been through the
bathroom a million times, no one ever discovered his
hiding place. No one ever figured out that he'd been in
the room, watching and hearing everything.

jerry's big party

Stanley put his dad's knife away, but he kept his Dark Man mask on as he climbed into the laundry hamper. One could never be too careful when dealing with vampires, space aliens, and other assorted denizens of the dark. There was one other rather amazing quality that the laundry hamper possessed, Stanley had noticed: It was never empty. Mrs. Olsen, his fifth-grade teacher, had read a story in class about this poor family who'd been given a magic pitcher of milk, and no matter how much they drank, it always stayed filled. Stanley thought that the laundry hamper might somehow be in the same category. His mom would probably know the answer to this puzzle, only Stanley didn't think it was a good idea to ask her. His mom, he figured, wouldn't quite appreciate a never-ending flow of laundry, even if it was a miracle.

Another great thing about the laundry hamper was its extra-large size—his mom always said that clothes got dirty just from the thought of being worn by Jerry and him. So she'd bought a superlarge hamper nearly the size of a washing machine, only it was made from woven bamboo, so you could see through the sides. At least, from the inside you could see through the sides; from the outside all you could see was absolutely nothing, which was exactly the point. He was invisible and protected, even when asleep.

And that was where his mom found him when they came home early, looking for Jerry. Or actually, that was where she didn't find him. "Oh, my goodness!" Stanley heard her yelling. "Stanley's gone too! Stanley!" she shouted. "Stanley!" He heard his mom running from room to room, then a pounding on the bathroom door. "Stanley, are you in there!"

"Just a second," Stanley said, his voice somewhat muffled. He scrambled up out of the hamper, then flushed the toilet for effect. "I'm coming, I'm coming!" he said as his mom knocked again. At least she didn't barge right in, like Jimmy's mom did. Stanley never dared use the bathroom at Jimmy's house.

For a second his mom looked as though she was going to hug and kiss him. But instead, she puckered her nose and said, "Stanley, did you take your shower tonight?" Then her face changed, hardening. Stanley felt her fingers biting into his arms as she bent down. "Do you know where your brother went?" He shook his head, staring at the floor. "Don't lie to me," she warned. "Mrs. Lanorsky called us at the club and told us that Jerry left in your father's car. Did you have anything to do with this?" Stanley shrugged and tried to wiggle away, but his mother took his chin in her hand, forcing him to look at her. "I sincerely hope not, young man," she said, "because boys who steal cars get sent away to reform school."

"Is that what's going to happen to Jerry?" Stanley blurted out.

His mom stood up. "You just get into your bed," she told him. "And stay there!"

Stanley got into bed, but he bounded over to the heating vent, listening intently as soon as he heard his mom's footsteps echoing down the hall. He imagined his mom and dad in the living room, sitting in their favorite opposite chairs, arms crossed, waiting in the dark. For sure he knew that the lights were off because he heard his mom tell his dad that they would just sit there in the dark until the "little miscreant comes home." Stanley quickly crawled back to the pile of clothes next to his bed, feeling through them until he found his pocket notebook and his red pen. *M-i-s-c-r-e-a-n-t,* he wrote, using the glow of the fish tank above his bed—he didn't dare turn on the lights. Then he crawled back to the vent.

For a while Stanley thought about how lonely Jerry would be living in a reform school and how maybe he could send Dark Man with him, even though Jerry didn't believe in Dark Man. Dark Man didn't like Jerry all that much either, to tell the truth. Then Stanley heard the sound of his dad's car pulling into the driveway.

"Are we having a party?" Jerry said when he walked into the living room.

"A party?" his dad yelled, and Stanley didn't need the vent to hear him. *"A party?"*

Then he heard his mom say, "Please, I'll handle this." And Stanley didn't need the vent to hear her, either. She yelled at Jerry for a while about how embarrassed she was and how everyone now knew what a rotten kid they had since they had had to leave the club and how no one else's kids ever did such rotten things. She went on and on until her voice started getting hoarse. That was when his dad took over again.

"I work my butt off," he yelled at Jerry, "and do you know why? To make sure you kids have everything you could want. Maybe you think I like working, huh? Well, I do not! Not if this is what I get for it!" For a minute everything got quiet, but Stanley knew that was only because his dad was catching his breath. His dad smoked, and it was hard for him to yell for more than a minute or two, on account of, as his mom had told them, the cigarettes had shrunk his lungs. His mom also smoked, only her cigarettes were thinner and they had a filter, which was why she could yell for so much longer, Stanley figured. "Well, this is it, buddy boy!" his dad finally said. "The last straw, the final inning—"

"The tip of the iceberg?" Jerry interrupted. "No, sorry, that doesn't work. The bottom of the barrel?" Stanley heard the loud bang of his dad's fist hammering the table next to his chair and then the sound of his dad's glass ashtray tumbling onto the carpet. "Sorry," Jerry said. "Just trying to be helpful."

"Everything's a joke to you," his mom said. "Well, maybe this time the joke's on you. Tell him, Irving."

Stanley cringed—his mom almost never called his dad by his name. "Things are going to change around here, that's what your mom and I have decided," his dad announced. "First thing tomorrow I'm going to make some phone calls, find out what we can do with you. Then we'll see, buddy boy! Then we'll see. Maybe you think there's some law that says we have to keep you."

"Actually, Dad, I think there is a law—"

Stanley heard another bang on the table. "Just give me that car key and go to your room! And don't open the door till I say it can open!"

Stanley dived back into bed and under the covers, practicing his snoring. He wondered where his dad would send Jerry and if he would have to go with him and if his dad would make them pay back the $17,350 he said it cost to raise them each year. Also, he worried about whether the $17,350 included interest or not. And then there was inflation to think about. Stanley wished he had his calculator with him.

After ten minutes or so, though Stanley wasn't even close to suffocation, he opened up an airhole in his covers. The record for staying under the covers without an airhole was nearly an hour . . . or something like that—staying-under-the-covers records were rather complicated in that the outside and inside air temperatures had to be taken into consideration. He usually just let the people at ESPN figure it out. But Stanley didn't want to set a record just then, he wanted to tell Jerry that no matter where he got sent, Stanley would call every day. Unless there wasn't a phone, of course. If there wasn't a phone, he'd write. Maybe not every day—even a speed writer like Stanley might not be able to write every day. But once every week or two, for sure.

"Jerry," he whispered. No one answered. "Jerry," he whispered again, louder this time. Stanley listened intently. In the dead silence of the room the soft squeak of the window above his brother's bed sliding open sounded as loud as the hunting cry of a famished vampire. "Jerry!" But it was too late. The dim glow of the fish tank illuminated Jerry's shoulders and grinning face as he slipped backward out the window. A few moments after that Stanley heard the sound of his dad's car starting up again, tires crunching against the pavement as it pulled into the street.

beachfront property in madagascar

The next morning Stanley didn't wait for anyone to tell him to get out of the house; he left as soon as he heard his dad yelling at the man on the phone. "What do you mean we have to keep him?" his dad roared. "You're telling me there really is a law? . . . What? The only way you can take him is if someone files a complaint about us? About *us*? What about *him*?"

Stanley didn't like to stay in on Sunday mornings, anyway. There wasn't much to watch on TV, and besides, Sunday mornings were an excellent time to set records. He could kick rocks, jump walkways, and even attempt daring land-speed records on his ultrasonic bike—all with perfect concentration, on account of the streets were deserted and Stanley didn't have to worry about anyone discovering his secret identity. But not today. Today he needed to go visit Uncle Willie. Alone.

Stanley had gone to the convalescent hospital every week for two months, but never alone. His mom had always driven him. The problem was that his mom always ended up yelling at Uncle Willie on account of Uncle Willie didn't want to be Uncle Willie anymore. He wanted to be someone named Alan Ladd. In fact, he said he *was* Alan Ladd, which was why the hospital wouldn't let him go home. "Idolization amnesia," the doctor called it—Uncle Willie couldn't remember who he was, so he'd become someone else.

"But who's Alan Ladd?" Stanley had asked his mom on one of the trips to the hospital.

She sighed. "Alan Ladd was a movie star many years ago. I think he died in an auto accident. He was handsome and dashing and brave and—well, Uncle Willie could certainly *use* a bit of Alan Ladd. He just can't *be* Alan Ladd."

"And why not?" Uncle Willie had smiled when Stanley told him what his mom had said. "After all, the last time I checked, the world was certainly in need of a few more Alan Ladds. Just call me a volunteer."

That was when his mom had started yelling and saying how selfish and thoughtless it was for Uncle Willie to throw away everything he'd worked for. But the new Uncle Willie had just laughed. And not the little, cover-your-mouth-with-your-hand laugh that Uncle Willie used to have. No, not even close! The new Alan Ladd Uncle Willie had spread his arms wide, thrown his head back, and let go with a rumble of laughter that filled the room to overflowing, echoing off the walls. At first the other patients had just smiled, but when Uncle Willie didn't stop, they began laughing along with him. And when his mom had tried to shush Uncle Willie, he'd even picked her up, swinging her around in circles, like he really *was* a movie star. Not only that, but the other patients had joined in, clapping out a beat, stamping their feet, and hooting. Stanley wasn't absolutely positive, but he thought he might have even seen his mom start to smile. Of course, that was before she got really mad and said she wasn't ever coming back to visit again.

An entire month had gone by since then, and Stanley was pretty sure that his mom meant it when she said she wasn't going to visit again. So if Stanley wanted to see Uncle Willie, he had to walk. Which meant . . . the Snake Canyon trail. There simply was no other way to get past the freeway. Stanley had never actually been in Snake Canyon, which ran under the freeway; all he really knew was that Jerry and Alvin caught rattlesnakes there and were always inviting him along. They said he'd make great rattlesnake bait. As he climbed down the steep embankment used to reach the canyon bottom, Stanley hoped they were only kidding. Not that it mattered. Kidding or not, he had to get to the hospital. He had to know how Uncle Willie had done it—how he'd become someone else.

Stanley remembered exactly what his uncle had said that night they had broken down the bathroom door, on account of he'd been there, hiding in the laundry hamper. None of his parents' friends ever used that bathroom, so Stanley had been surprised when his uncle had come in, locking the door behind him. "I mean, just what is the point?" Uncle Willie had yelled. "Answer me that, would you?" For a moment Stanley had tried to think of an answer—actually, it wasn't that hard, it was a question he asked himself all the time, especially during school. But then he realized that his uncle wasn't talking to him.

"Unlock this door immediately, Willie!" his mother said from the other side. "Stop acting like a fool!"

"But that's the whole point. I am a fool! I can't even

talk to a girl! I'm useless! Hopeless! Pathetic!" His uncle slammed his hand onto the counter, so hard that Stanley jumped.

"Willie, you're scaring me! If you don't come out this instant, I'm calling the police. Do you want to ruin the entire evening for everyone?"

"Oh, sure, just come out and play nice! Just be a good little Willie! I don't need a mother anymore, sis. I need . . . I need . . . I need a personality transplant! That's it!" his uncle said, pointing to the image of himself in the mirror. "I don't have to be Willie the Wormlike if I don't want to be. *And I don't want to be!*" he shouted. *"End of discussion!"*

Through the bamboo of the hamper, Stanley could see his uncle pick up the electric shaver that Jerry had borrowed from Alvin Bagley, slapping it against his hand, harder and harder. "I'm talking to the police right now," Stanley heard his mom say. "A car's almost here. Is that what you want?" Willie banged the shaver on the edge of the sink but said nothing. "You answer me, Willie!" his mom shouted. "Answer me!"

"Here's an answer!" he shouted back. Uncle Willie raised the shaver, aiming it at the mirror. That was when he'd slipped, falling backward, his head banging loudly against the side of the tub. It was all Stanley's fault, really—his mom was always telling him how dangerous it was to leave water on the floor after a bath. Stanley wanted to get out of the hamper and help his uncle, only that was when the police arrived.

"Hurry!" Stanley heard his mom shouting, then heavy footsteps pounding down the hall. "I think he's done something!"

"Please step out of the way," an unfamiliar voice said. Then the door burst open, and two police officers rushed in, followed closely by Stanley's mom and dad. He heard his mom scream and a police officer say, "Back up, everyone! Give us some room!" Stanley closed his eyes and put his hands over his ears, sinking deeper into the laundry.

Stanley stayed as close to the middle of the canyon bottom's dirt path as possible. He gathered a handful of rocks, but he didn't know whether to toss them at the bushes ahead or not. At the zoo, in the World's Biggest Reptile House, none of the snakes had bushes to hide in, so Stanley didn't know for sure if snakes even liked to hide in bushes. What he did know was that if he were a snake, especially a hungry one looking for a kid to bite, he would sure hide in a bush. But would a well-aimed rock scare them away or just make them angry? It was funny how no one ever wrote about the things in life a person really needed to know.

Stanley finally decided that the best way to avoid hungry snakes was to hop—not only would it confuse them, but hopping would make it sound like he weighed a whole lot more than he did. Anyway, he didn't get bitten, though he almost died of embarrassment when some kids standing on the freeway overpass hooted at him. Of course, they probably would have hooted even more if he'd stopped hopping and all the snakes that'd been following him chose that moment to attack.

Stanley didn't stop at the reception desk of the hospital, but marched right past, hurrying toward the rest room. It was a trick he'd learned from Robby Lanorsky; nobody ever stopped a kid if he was hurrying toward the rest room. Besides that, he was pretty dusty and sweaty from hopping the whole way.

Uncle Willie was in his usual spot in what the sign above the door said was the visitors' lounge. It was a large room, with glass picture windows looking out over the city and plenty of tables and chairs and even couches. Not that Uncle Willie was sitting down—he almost never sat down. Not the new Uncle Willie, at least. He was laughing and gesturing with his hands, telling a group of people about the time he'd visited Egypt and run into a mummy smuggler. Stanley never even knew his uncle had been to Egypt. Of course, the old Uncle Willie never told stories about where he went on his business trips. He just said that they were too boring to talk about.

Stanley wanted to wait until Uncle Willie had finished the story and everyone had left, but when his uncle saw him, he said, "Stop the presses! Hold everything! I've just spotted my former nephew, the stupendous Stanley Krakow! And"—he glanced about the room, searching—"unaccompanied by the Lady Krakow! Now, *this* is a story waiting to be told! Come up here, my brave young man."

Staring at the floor and feeling his face turn bright red, Stanley walked up to where his uncle was standing. "Hello!" His uncle smiled brightly, bending to shake Stanley's hand. "And what brings you out into the wild world all alone?"

"Well . . ." Now that he was there, Stanley didn't really know how to begin. How, exactly, did you ask a person about how they had become someone else?

"Cat got your tongue?" Uncle Willie asked. "Hey, that's no good!" His uncle began dancing, his feet shuffling out a rhythm, his arms swinging, fingers snapping. "You have to learn to speak up, son!" Then he started to sing: "Speak up, say what you want! Speak up, say what you feel! Don't wait for the world to approve you, 'cause don't you know it just never will." Uncle Willie twirled down, spinning in a circle onto his knees, coming to rest with his arms wide in front of Stanley, ready to give him a hug. His mom was always telling him to speak up, but it sure never sounded like that! Around him people applauded, then they stepped back to let them talk.

"Well . . ." Stanley smiled shyly. He took a deep breath, then blurted out, in one long rush, "You used to be Uncle Willie, but now you're not him anymore, you're someone else, only I forgot your new name—oh, yeah, it's Alan Ladd, but even if it is Alan Ladd . . . what do I call you?" When his uncle didn't answer right away, Stanley added, "That's only the first thing I want to know."

"I see," Uncle Willie said, nodding his head. "You know, you're the first person who's actually *asked* me what I prefer to be called. Everyone else just calls me Willie, despite . . . well, nothing against your old uncle Willie, it's just that I'm not him. Not anymore. And if that's not okay with them, well, then they'll just have to keep me locked up here forever! I'll write a book! I'll organize the inmates! I'll—" He stopped abruptly, staring at Stanley. "But back to the question. Alan's the name, and Alan's what I prefer to be called."

"Alan?" Stanley said, testing out the sound. It felt . . . wrong. "Just Alan?" he added.

"Doesn't quite work for you," Uncle Willie said, scratching his head, "I can see that." For a moment he frowned, thinking. Then he smiled again, clapping his hands. "How about I be your Uncle Alan? How's that? I'll simply adopt you as a nephew. We can draw up the appropriate and necessary papers right now, with no one the wiser! I need only to know your full legal name."

"Uncle Alan," Stanley murmured, and then louder, because he liked the sound of it. "Uncle Alan." Stanley beamed. He didn't care what his mom and dad said, he liked the new Uncle Willie—Uncle Alan—much better than the old one. Especially if people would still say they were a lot alike. "Stanley Uriah Krakow," he answered.

Uncle Alan sat down at an empty table, motioning Stanley to join him. He took a small notebook from his coat pocket, wrote in it for a minute, then ripped out a page. It read: *I, Alan Ladd, do hereby and forthwith officially adopt Stanley Uriah Krakow as my nephew.* Beneath that it was signed, *Alan Ladd.* "Now you have to sign it. After that keep it in a safe place." He leaned forward, whispering, "You're my only heir, and I'm worth a bundle!"

Stanley signed the paper and stuck it in his pocket. But then he didn't exactly know how to go on. Usually, when Stanley didn't know how to say something, he just didn't say anything. Only this time he had no choice. "How did you get to be someone else?" he finally asked. "I mean, how can I do it? You know, become someone else?"

Uncle Willie—Uncle Alan now—laughed uproariously. "Now, there's a question!" he managed to say. There were tears in his eyes, he was laughing so hard. "If you ever figure that out, you won't need my money—you'll be rich all by your lonesome. The problem is, Stanley, my man, I never learned to be someone else. I just got sick and tired of being someone I wasn't. And presto! I decided to become who I really was!"

Stanley sat back in the chair, deflated. He already knew who he was, and he didn't much like him. He wanted to sing and dance like the new Uncle Willie and to have people gather around him to listen to his stories. That's what he wanted. Now all he had to look forward to was a long hike home. With the snakes waiting for him. He was too tired to hop all the way, a fact he was sure the snakes were counting on. "I don't suppose you know anything about snakes?" he muttered hopelessly.

Uncle Alan smiled. "Do I know about snakes? Why, next to Adam, I'm probably the world's expert in snakology. Did I ever tell you about the time I was shipwrecked in Madagascar? Madagascar, by the way, is the snake capital of the world. The deadly snake capital of the world," he added, rising from his knees as he began his story. "It was summertime when my ship went down, a summer storm got her, a gust of wind so strong, it literally picked the ship up, blew her twenty feet off the waves. I was the only one to survive—and that only because a Madagascan red-eyed eagle, largest bird in the world, thought he might as well grab a snack before the rest of the crew became fish food." People began to wander over, listening. Uncle Willie paused for a moment, letting them come nearer. "Like I was telling my nephew, Stanley, who's thinking of becoming a snake charmer," Stanley's uncle began again, "beachfront property isn't worth much in Madagascar, not with the snakes waiting on the beach for shipwrecked survivors. Luckily for me, the eagle lost its grip on me just over a Poombah village, probably the only place in all of Madagascar where snakes won't go. The problem was, who wants to live in a Poombah village for the rest of their natural life? That's when I learned about Poombah sticks. Let me tell you . . ."

On Stanley's way home there were still kids on the freeway overpass, and they still hooted at him as he walked underneath, swinging his Poombah stick into the bushes. He ignored them. "Poombah!" he shouted. It was a secret Madagascan word used to frighten snakes. After leaving the hospital Stanley had found a stick just like the one Uncle Alan had described, a Poombah stick. "Poombah!" he yelled again. Above him he imagined the hoots turning to cheers. "Poombah, I say! Poombah!"

theresa wasnicki's welcome

On Monday morning Stanley was up even before his father. He shoveled his usual breakfast—Trix—into his mouth in huge gulps, drinking in the last couple of mouthfuls without even noticing the colors. Grabbing his book bag and hurrying out the door, Stanley wondered if this oversight would wreck the scientific study he was doing. So far he had written down the last surviving color of Trix for thirty-eight days in a row. Red was way ahead, even though there weren't any more reds in the box than other colors. Stanley knew this to be true because he opened each new box before any had been eaten and he counted. He could only conclude that there was something special about the color itself, which was the reason he'd spent half his allowance the week before on red ballpoint pens.

Unfortunately for the future of science, he had to be at school especially early that morning. Not only did he have to write *I will pay attention in class* one hundred times, but he had to write *I will not wad up pieces of paper and shoot them at the window* one hundred times also. This was because on Friday, Mrs. Olsen had caught him making maps of the lost world of Zambor during math, and then, during history, he had tried to stop a secret attack of ants by shooting spitballs into the window cracks. Everyone should have cheered him for being such a hero, but no, they just laughed when he hadn't noticed Mrs. Olsen sneaking up on him and had shot her in the bosom by mistake.

The absolutely most horrible part of writing anything one hundred times for Mrs. Olsen was that it had to be legible. Mrs. Olsen actually read all one hundred sentences! Talk about not having a life! The only thing worse than being Mrs. Olsen, Stanley supposed, was being Mr. Olsen. He could just imagine their dinner conversation: *Honey, let me just read you*

Stanley's newest assignment, titled "I Will Pay Attention in Class."

Stanley had planned to complete his assignments at home that weekend, but then, after the car incident, his mom had grounded Jerry forever and told his brother that if he didn't get home within ten minutes after school, he might as well never come home. They would just change all the locks and call the police and have Jerry taken away until the end of time. Under the circumstances, Stanley had decided that he would complete the assignments at school, thus avoiding the possibility of his mom finding them. After all, his mom had supernatural radar abilities when it came to finding things Stanley didn't want found. Besides, he had a perfect place for completing last-minute assignments before school—the boys' rest room, on account of he could lock himself in a stall and everyone would leave him alone. Naturally, he was a world-record holder in writing almost anything one hundred times. Even while sitting on a toilet.

Stanley skidded expertly into the bike rack, locking up his bike almost before his feet hit the ground and then sprinting for the boys' rest room. He hit the door running, nearly breaking his nose when it didn't open. Fortunately, the ESPN van hadn't yet arrived, so there would be no pictures of the Famous Stanley Krakow picking himself up off the ground in total defeat. He tried the door again. No doubt about it, the door was locked. Stanley brushed the dirt off his pants, wondering how he could possibly save himself. Kids would start arriving at school any minute; he needed a place to complete his assignments. That was when he remembered another thing he liked about the school rest rooms: There were never any teachers in them, for the very good reason that teachers had their own rest rooms.

Stanley felt his hands trembling as he walked toward the teachers' rest rooms. It didn't matter, he had no choice. If he didn't get his assignments done, Mrs. Olsen would send him to the principal, and the principal would call his mother, and his mother would change all the locks and call the police and have him taken away until the end of time. He took a deep breath as he neared the men's rest room, then pretended to slip on a banana peel, just the way he'd seen it done on TV. The door banged open as he fell into the room.

After rolling enough times to check the place out Stanley got up. He was alone! He wanted to shout, but instead, he hurried into a toilet stall, locked the door, and began writing. It would have worked, too, if only Mr. Hardin, the principal, hadn't come in. There was no mistaking who it was, on account of he was singing, and nobody sang as badly as the principal. He was practically famous for it. Once he'd even been on TV, on a show that gave prizes for the very worst perform-ance. Mr. Hardin would have won, too, if only this lady's dog, who was doing a dead dog act, hadn't really died. The lady had started crying and wailing, and of course they had to give her the prize, in order just to get her to drag her dead dog off the stage.

With his legs pulled up and the stall door locked, Stanley continued writing, trying not to let Mr. Hardin's terrible singing slow him down. He still had plenty of time, and sooner or later, Mr. Hardin would have to leave. Wouldn't he?

Stanley sat upright so quickly that he thought Mr. Hardin would hear. Not that it would matter, for Stanley realized with a cold shudder that Mr. Hardin was the only person in the entire school who could stay in the rest room after the bell rang. After all, he was the principal. The principal didn't need to be in class. The principal could wash his hands and sing all day long and no one would miss him! Stanley wanted to cry. He looked at his carefully written assignments, at each carefully written line, and knew, without a doubt, that it wouldn't matter. Mrs. Olsen wouldn't be reading them, wouldn't be commenting on how very legible it all was, because there was nothing in the world that Mrs. Olsen hated more than tardiness. Tardiness meant an immediate trip to the principal's office, where the principal would discover that Stanley was guilty of almost everything there was to be guilty of—tardiness, spying, and impersonating an adult, just for starters.

The bell rang, but Mr. Hardin didn't leave until he had mangled most of another song. Twenty seconds later Stanley was at the door to his classroom, inching it open, praying that Mrs. Olsen wouldn't notice. That was impossible, of course; Mrs. Olsen, even though she was nearly one hundred years old, possessed superpower abilities when it came to kids sneaking in after the bell had rung. The only reason there wasn't a comic book about her amazing powers was that no kid would be stupid enough to pay money for a comic-book superhero whose only ability was getting kids in trouble. Besides, even if she miraculously didn't notice him, it was a sure thing that Steve Klemp, the only kid in fifth grade who shaved and who hated Stanley worse than anybody, would let Mrs. Olsen know.

But she didn't notice. Steve Klemp didn't either. In fact, no one noticed on account of everyone was staring at the front of the classroom, where the same girl who'd waved at Stanley from the moving van was standing toe-to-toe with Mrs. Olsen. "I don't care what the stupid report card says," the girl said firmly. "I ought to know how to spell my own name!" She took the chalk out of Mrs. Olsen's hand and turned to the blackboard, where Mrs. Olsen had written, *Please welcome a new student, Teresa Waznicki.* "It's Theresa with an 'h,'" the girl said, adding an "h," "and Wasnicki with an 's.'" She drew a line through the "z" and added an "s."

"But . . . but . . . but . . ." For the first time in recorded history Mrs. Olsen didn't have a thing to say. Stanley slid noiselessly into the room, inching toward his seat.

"I tried to tell you," the new girl, Theresa Wasnicki, said. "I was only at my last school for two months. We move a lot."

Mrs. Olsen stared at the report card in her hand, then at Theresa Wasnicki, then at the report card. "Well," she finally said, "you will just have to go to the office, young lady, until this is straightened out. I cannot admit you into class with your name not correctly spelled, now can I?"

"Some welcome!" Theresa Wasnicki said, then grabbed the report card and marched out of the classroom.

For a moment the class was absolutely silent. Then

Steve Klemp said, "Hey, I guess we don't need a spelling lesson today, huh, Mrs. Olsen?" Everyone started laughing, but they immediately stopped when Mrs. Olsen grabbed her yardstick and smashed it down an inch away from Steve Klemp's hand.

"Now, class, where were we?" Mrs. Olsen said, as if nothing had happened. "Oh, yes." She turned to Stanley. "You have something for me, I believe, Mr. Krakow?"

Stanley raised his two assignments into the air, holding his breath as Mrs. Olsen took them. "Very legible," she muttered, her eyes darting back and forth over the lines. "Yes, very legible, indeed." Mrs. Olsen smiled down at him, so close that Stanley could see the glue that held in her false teeth. At least, Stanley hoped it was glue. "I do believe this has taught you a lesson?" she said. Stanley nodded sincerely, though probably the lesson he'd learned wasn't quite the one Mrs. Olsen was meaning. The important part, he thought, was that he was learning. That's what school was all about, wasn't it?

"And now, class," Mrs. Olsen announced, beaming and walking back to the front of the class, "it's reading-aloud period!"

Stanley almost gagged. He'd totally forgotten to chart where he was on the reading-aloud list! Usually,

if there was even the slightest possibility of him reading, he stayed home sick, which was easy, since even
the thought of standing up in front of the entire class
made him want to throw up. "Let's see," Mrs. Olsen
said. "Today we start with . . . Emily Mendosa."

Yes! Stanley thought. *Saved by alphabetical order!*
Stanley wondered if there was a world record for how
many times a kid could be saved in a single day. He
opened his reader and paid perfect attention, not
wanting to press his luck.

But the empty seat two rows over—where the new
girl, Theresa Wasnicki, was supposed to be sitting—
kept pulling at his eyes. Stanley wondered if maybe he
should thank her when she came back into class. After
all, it was because of her that he'd been rescued from
the principal's office. But even as he thought it, he
knew he never would. He'd never have the courage. So
it was just as well that she didn't come back into class
that day.

a chance meeting

At the final bell Stanley didn't rush out with all the other kids. He packed his books, pens, pencils, erasers, ruler, and notebook carefully into his book bag and even more carefully walked out of the classroom. It had been a nearly perfect day, and he certainly didn't want to ruin it now. To top it all off, Robby had rented Stanley's bike for a quarter, on account of Robby's had a flat tire and he didn't want to be late getting home for his Little League game. Stanley didn't play Little League—first of all, because he was too shy, and second, because his amazing talent would have given away his secret identity.

Walking across the school playground, Stanley spotted the ESPN van parked across the street. It looked quite similar to the Persons' van, and it even appeared that Mrs. Person, Blake's mom, was sitting in the driver's seat; but Stanley knew better. Mondays were always a little slow for ESPN, which is why they liked to follow him home, filming his attempts to set Rock Kicking records. Stanley was well aware that Rock Kicking wasn't the most exciting of sports, except that he was the all-time, absolute world-record holder. In the world of Rock Kicking, he was a legend.

Stanley had even found a way home that no other kids ever used, in order to protect his secret identity. Of course, he had had to sneak back into the class-room a few times during lunch and go through Mrs. Olsen's desk files for addresses, but it had been worth the risk. In the end, Stanley had been able to mark out on a street map the address of every kid in his class and their probable routes home, all in easy-to-follow red ink. After that all he needed to do was find a way that avoided all the streets marked with red. The amazing part was that it worked! He wanted to turn the whole project in for extra credit, but that would be a sure way of blowing his secret identity. Also, Mrs. Olsen might begin to wonder just how he'd gotten his information.

Stanley walked three blocks in not exactly the right direction to reach the ESPN Rock-Kicking course. Like any good professional, he used the extra time wisely, picking out a few well-formed rocks to kick. "You're only as good as your tools," he often told the reporters. "Concentration is the key." And it was true. The rules of Rock Kicking were very complicated— first a right-foot kick, then a left, alternating as he went. A minimum of twenty successful kicks in a row was required, with no running at the rock, no kicking the rock off the sidewalk, and a maximum of two kicks to cross a street. As most people in the world knew, Stanley held the record of twenty-one steps per kick. No other competitor was even close.

After the first couple of blocks, when the cars started to thin out and he didn't have to worry about smashing headlights, Stanley revved it up. One tremendous kick skipped onto the street, then back onto the sidewalk. Forty-three steps! He could actually hear people inside their houses cheering. Checking to see that the street was clear, Stanley bowed to the car he figured had the camera in it. In Rock-Kicking circles he was known for his politeness. Too bad his mom didn't follow Rock Kicking.

Unfortunately for the record books, Stanley totally

missed his first kick across Linden Avenue, and his second kick, though powerful enough, hit the curb and bounced back into the street. Disqualified. Stanley smiled to hide his disappointment. He pulled another rock out of his pants pocket and tried again. It skipped perfectly across the street, jumping the curb and sailing onto the sidewalk—a great kick until it swerved into a hedge lining the sidewalk. Hedges were uncommon right next to the sidewalk, and the rules allowed him to place his rock back on the sidewalk, if only he could find it. There was a ten-step penalty, of course.

The problem was, he couldn't find his rock. The hedge was thick, and though he bent down and looked, he couldn't see his rock. At last he crawled in, carefully moving his hands over the dried leaves lining the ground. Stanley suddenly realized that his bottom was sticking out of the hedge and that the cameras were probably filming it. He quickly moved farther into the bushes, right against the chain-link fence on the other side. And that was when he saw her. Theresa Wasnicki.

She was on her hands and knees, just like he was, about twenty feet away on the grass lawn below her porch. Cutting the grass with a pair of scissors. Stanley rubbed his eyes and shook his head, then looked again. Yes, that was what she was doing, snapping at the grass with a pair of old, rusted scissors. And not looking very happy about it either. In fact, Stanley could see tears on her cheeks.

"What exactly do you think you're doing?" a woman said, her voice harsh and biting. For a moment Stanley thought he'd been caught, but then he realized the woman was talking to Theresa, speaking from the porch above where Theresa was working. It was the same woman who'd been squishing Theresa against the window in the moving van. "This is supposed to be work, not play!"

"But, Mom, this is impossible! These stupid scissors don't even cut!"

"Don't blame the scissors! It's not them that's stupid, it's you! Why'd you have to tell them your name was spelled wrong, anyway? It's been good enough for the last five schools! Now I have to dig through all of creation for your birth certificate! You think I don't have better things to do?" Theresa said nothing. Her mom couldn't see the face she was making, but Stanley could. "You get this whole yard done. I don't care if it takes you all night!" Theresa's mom waited a moment, then stomped her foot down hard on the porch floor.

"Okay, okay!" Theresa said. "I hear you!"

"And?"

"I'll get it done, okay?" She returned to snipping at

the grass, faster and faster, tears streaming down her face. "I'll get it done!"

Stanley's hand closed on his rock. He backed onto the sidewalk, crouching as he walked past their house, hoping the hedge would hide him. All he could think of was that he didn't want to be seen, not by Theresa Wasnicki, and certainly not by her mother.

10

stanleystein

There were times in the past when Stanley had gone days and days without getting into trouble at school, so he didn't think much of it when the final bell rang the next day without Mrs. Olsen sending him to the principal or having him write something one hundred times on the board or even being told to pay attention. Wednesday, too, passed without a single incident. Maybe it was that he kept thinking of Jerry and of how, any day now, he might get sent away forever. Also, if Jerry messed up and his mom changed all the locks, would anyone remember to give him a new key? Probably not, which was why Stanley had borrowed one of his dad's screwdrivers and unscrewed the lock on the window above his bed. You couldn't tell that it was unscrewed, of course, on account of it sat in the same place as always, right at the top of the bottom window. Stanley even put a little glue on it, to make sure that it didn't move. The problem was, every night he had to screw it back in. It was one thing to fool his mom and dad during the day, but he could hardly count on vampires, zombies, and aliens being so inattentive.

However, when Thursday passed without any trouble, Stanley began to wonder just what was going on. Had the old Mrs. Olsen somehow been transmogrified into a newer, kinder version of herself? He doubted if even God could accomplish that feat. Still, he supposed it was possible. To find out, Stanley paid perfect attention from the second he walked into class on Friday, watching every move Mrs. Olsen made. It didn't take long. In the first ten minutes of class she broke her ruler over Steve Klemp's reading book, she caught Sylvie Atwater passing a note and read it to the whole class, and she yelled at Jimmy for fidgeting. So much for God working wonders.

Suddenly, in the middle of Mrs. Olsen reading one of her favorite poems, Stanley sat bolt upright, gulping loudly as he realized that there was another possibility: What if he wasn't being good at all? What if someone had somehow, totally without his knowledge, turned him invisible? Stanley gulped again, even louder. Mrs. Olsen, who allowed absolutely no noise during her poetry readings, said nothing to him. Well, she couldn't very well say anything to him if she couldn't see him, could she? Now that he had thought of it, he was amazed that he hadn't thought of it earlier. How else to explain his perfect week? He tried to recall if his mom had noticed him. Or his dad, or Jerry, or anyone. All he could remember was kicking rocks and setting speed records on his bike and avoiding Theresa Wasnicki on account of he was ashamed to have seen her crying. Thinking back, hadn't it been just a little too easy to avoid her?

But why would anyone turn him invisible? Stanley tried to tell himself that he was being silly, but then his heart plummeted into his stomach as he realized the terrible, horrible, but all-too-obvious truth: One of his rivals for his ESPN contract had done it! After all, ESPN couldn't very well televise his world records or interview him if he was invisible. It all made perfect sense!

The recess bell sounded, but instead of running out to the playground with everyone else, Stanley walked slowly into the boys' rest room. He stared at himself in the mirror for a long time, turning first one way, then the other. He certainly appeared to be all there, but then, he didn't know all that much about being invisible. He couldn't remember anything in the *Encyclopædia Britannica* about it, so he supposed it was possible that invisible people were invisible only to others, not to themselves. It seemed as though his parents would have said something about him being gone—but then again, he was usually pretty quiet, so maybe they hadn't noticed. Now, if Jerry had disappeared, that would have been a big deal!

Just then Jimmy walked in. Jimmy didn't say hello or notice Stanley at all, but Jimmy never said hello to Stanley. Still, if he was truly invisible . . . He walked up slowly behind Jimmy, who was using the sink to wash his hands. Stanley waved his arms around, careful to make no noise. All Jimmy did was squirt more soap onto his hands and continue staring into the mirror, his face blank. Next, Stanley moved his arms out to his sides and tottered from leg to leg, like Frankenstein would do, closer and closer. If Stanley was visible, Jimmy would jump away or turn around. Or something! But Jimmy didn't do a thing; he just continued washing his hands, occasionally glancing up at the mirror.

Then George and Robby walked in, along with a bunch of other kids. "Look at what your dumb dweeb friend is doing," Jimmy said as he reached for a paper towel. He turned around, moving past Stanley, still ignoring him. "Frankenstein comes to Nerdsville."

Except for Robby, the rest of the kids started to laugh. One of them called out, "Stanleystein," and soon everyone was chanting, "Stanleystein, Stanleystein!" Stanley turned beet red, then buried his head beneath the faucet of the nearest sink.

When he finally looked up from the sink, Robby was the only one still in the bathroom. "Don't let Jimmy bother you," he said, patting Stanley on the shoulder. "He likes making fun of people. Only . . . what were you doing?" Robby started to laugh. "Man, Stan, you sure did look weird."

As he walked back to his class Stanley could see Jimmy already inside, posing in front of the whole class, tottering like Frankenstein, face twisted. Almost everyone was laughing, glancing back at Stanley's empty seat. Not Amy Fitzwaters, of course. Amy Fitzwaters never laughed at anything. Robby was in a different class, but Stanley would have bet that Robby wouldn't be laughing either. Everyone else was, though . . . except Stanley noticed that in the far corner Theresa Wasnicki wasn't laughing. That was probably because she was new. New kids didn't laugh much, Stanley had noticed. But she'd learn—it was always okay to laugh at Stanley, it was almost a class tradition. The moment Mrs. Olsen walked into the room, Stanley hurried for his seat, hoping no one would notice him. At least he didn't have to worry about being invisible anymore.

"Jimmy, would you care to visit Mr. Hardin?" Mrs. Olsen said. Jimmy immediately sat down. "Now, class, please open your math books to chapter eleven, and pay strict attention!"

Stanley did pay strict attention—at least, he did for the first ten minutes. The problem was, he'd already finished today's math lesson. In fact, Stanley had pretty much finished the rest of the book, all the way to the end of the year, which was only two weeks away. Usually, when Stanley had nothing to do during math period, he worked on math-related problems. That way, if Mrs. Olsen caught him, it at least looked like he was paying attention. On Fridays the problem he always worked on was if he'd have to stand up and read during reading-aloud period, which Mrs. Olsen scheduled for Monday mornings, on account of she couldn't think of a better way to ruin Stanley's weekend. This Friday, though, Stanley had already figured out that he was safe for the next Monday. After that there was only the last Monday of the school year, and no one, not even Mrs. Olsen, would ever have reading-aloud period on the last Monday of school.

So there was nothing for Stanley to do but stare at the clock above Mrs. Olsen's head, watching the second hand slowly click around the numbered face as he listened to a lesson he'd completed three weeks before. The clock was an official ESPN clock, of course, complete with a secret camera, placed there for no other reason than to record Stanley's attempts at the holding-your-breath world record. Obviously, no one knew that except Stanley. And he had to be very careful that no one ever would know. Even when he actually broke a record, the ESPN interviewers had to wait until school let out to interview him, so as not to expose his secret identity.

Stanley knew that the time was right for an attempt. Mrs. Olsen was jumping around, showing the class how integers related and not paying the least attention to him. And so, with one tremendous effort, Stanley sucked in most of the air in the room, holding it in his massive lungs, then tapped the secret code on his desktop, alerting the folks at ESPN. The clock camera would immediately be turned on and all ESPN programming interrupted, switched to his attempt. Stanley glanced casually at the clock, then sat back, doing his best to look cool for the camera.

The seconds ticked by, quickly at first, then ever more slowly and painfully as he neared the record—one minute forty-two seconds. At one minute his lungs finally got the idea that they were being put out of business; they began demanding action. Stanley clamped his teeth down hard over his lips. At one minute twenty his heart got into the act, thumping loudly for something to pump. At one minute thirty his insides began to burn, and he could almost feel the clock camera zoom in for a close-up of his contorted face, the commentators wondering just how long he could endure such torture.

"Stanley?" Mrs. Olsen moved in front of his desk, blocking the camera. With his last reserve of strength, Stanley twisted to the right, giving the camera a shot. "Stanley," Mrs. Olsen repeated, "I asked you a question. If it's not too much trouble, the class and I would be interested in your answer."

Naturally, Stanley couldn't answer, even if he did know what the question was, which he didn't. The Official Rules for Holding Your Breath were very strict, and once a contestant began, he couldn't take another breath for any reason, not even for answering Mrs. Olsen's questions. Besides, he was so near. One minute thirty-eight, one minute thirty-nine . . .

Two seconds before he reached the record, two

seconds before the entire world would have begun chanting his name, Mrs. Olsen broke her ruler across Stanley's desk. Stanley gasped, then fell sideways out of his desk, head on the floor and feet pumping the air. The class erupted into cheers, shouting, "Stanleystein, Stanleystein!" It took Mrs. Olsen nearly a minute to restore order and another minute to write a note to the principal.

no-pardon hardin

Stanley walked slower and slower as he neared the door to the principal's office, praying that it would be closed and locked. It wasn't, of course. The door to the principal's office was never closed, and Mr. Hardin was never absent. It was like he didn't have anything else to do; he spent his whole day staring at the door, waiting. Stanley had seen a program on TV about a certain type of snake that did the same thing. "No-Pardon Hardin" was what everyone called him, on account of no matter what anyone did, they got yelled at and sent to detention. One time Mrs. Olsen had sent Stanley to the office with a note saying that there was a bumblebee flying around in the classroom and would someone please come get it out. "What's this?" he'd shouted at Stanley. "A bumblebee? In your classroom? And just how did a bumblebee get into your classroom, Mr. Krakow? Can you please answer me that?" Mr. Hardin went on for about five minutes, until Steve Klemp came in with another note from Mrs. Olsen, asking what had happened to Stanley and how come no one was helping remove the bumblebee. "Hah!" he'd said to Steve Klemp. But he didn't yell. Even Mr. Hardin thought twice about yelling at Steve Klemp.

But this time there was no Steve Klemp, and Mr. Hardin wouldn't have to think even once about what to do with Stanley. Only there was no one in the principal's office. Stanley peeked in when his knock wasn't answered; no one was there. No one at all! For a moment Stanley considered returning to Mrs. Olsen's room, but what would that accomplish? Mrs. Olsen would just lecture him on the value of patience. Then she would write him another note and send Steve Klemp along with him to wait for the principal.

Stanley sat down where he always sat down, in the row of chairs facing Mr. Hardin's desk, and waited. After all, Mrs. Olsen had sent him to the principal's office, and that's where he was. There was a wall clock in the office, only it wasn't an official ESPN clock, so Stanley didn't even consider attempting any records. He looked around the room, but there wasn't much in it, just a desk and a row of chairs and a huge file cabinet. Stanley remembered that after each visit Mr. Hardin always said how he was going to write up a report on Stanley's behavior and how the report would follow Stanley from school to school and even after that, into the military or into a job. Stanley guessed that Mr. Hardin wrote reports on all the kids and that the huge file cabinet was where he kept them. Of course, the other kids' reports were probably not as long as Stanley's. Stanley got up from the chair and stepped toward the file cabinet.

The cabinet had five file drawers, with a ring of keys hanging from one of the keyholes. For a moment Stanley thought about finding his file, to see just what it was that would be following him around for the rest of his life. But then he realized that if the keys were still in the keyhole and the office door open, then Mr. Hardin would most probably be right back. That's all he needed, to get caught breaking into official school records. If that happened, Jerry would be the one calling *him* every day.

That was when he saw them, scrunched into a

dusty space between the file cabinet and the wall: another ring of keys. Without thinking, Stanley bent to pick them up. They were covered with dust and obviously had lain there for a very long time, but once Stanley had wiped them off, they appeared to be identical to the ones hanging from the file cabinet keyhole. Same shape, same number. Even the same colors.

"Well, well!" came a voice from behind Stanley. He immediately dropped both his hands into his pockets and spun around, facing Mr. Hardin. "And to what do I owe this pleasure?" Mr. Hardin asked.

"I, uh . . . I . . ."

Mr. Hardin marched to his desk and sat down, motioning Stanley to sit in one of the chairs. "Do you have a note, Mr. Krakow? Or is this a social visit?" He laughed grimly at his joke, fingers drumming on the desktop as he waited.

Stanley dug through his pockets. His fingers touched the key ring; he felt his face turning red. He wasn't going to give them back, that was for sure. Giving them back would just get him in more trouble. Finally, he found Mrs. Olsen's note in his back pocket and handed it over.

It took Mr. Hardin the rest of the period to go over the contents of Mrs. Olsen's note. "A regular plethora of rule breaking" was what he called it. Stanley wanted to take out his pocket notebook and write down *p-l-e-t-h-o-r-a*, but he somehow didn't think that Mr. Hardin would appreciate it.

The one and only good part of getting stuck in Mr. Hardin's office on a Friday was that Mr. Hardin didn't like to call parents up on Fridays, for if they requested a conference, he might have to stay late and mess up his weekend. As everyone knew, Mr. Hardin was single, so he wanted to get to a singles' bar as soon as possible—or at least that was what Steve Klemp said. Steve Klemp said that his father was always seeing Mr. Hardin at the singles' bars where he hung out, which Stanley thought was sort of odd because Steve Klemp's father wasn't single. Stanley always wanted to ask Steve Klemp about that, only he was worried that maybe Steve Klemp hadn't quite worked that part out yet. Since Steve Klemp was roughly the size of a gorilla, only without the natural intelligence to go with it, Stanley decided that it wouldn't be wise to upset him. Anyway, the important thing was that Mr. Hardin, for whatever reason, wasn't going to call his parents. And they wouldn't call the police and change the locks and have him taken away forever. At least, not that afternoon.

the death of pinocchio

Naturally, Robby didn't call the next morning, which was a Saturday. Of course, Stanley had taken the phone off the hook, but that was only because he didn't want to know that Robby hadn't called. Stanley figured that after what he'd done in the rest room on Friday, no one would ever call him again.

His dad came into the kitchen as Stanley was finishing his second bowl of Trix. He poured himself a cup of coffee, then sat heavily next to Stanley at the kitchen table, rubbing his face, which was still dark on account of he hadn't yet shaved. On Saturdays his dad didn't have to go to work until nine.

"Hi, Dad," Stanley said. His dad grunted, taking another sip from his coffee mug. Stanley stared at his cereal bowl. Three last Trix floated in the sea of milk. "Dad," he said, "I can't figure this out. Why are the red Trix always the last to get eaten?"

His dad looked up from his coffee mug, one eye pulling open to stare into Stanley's bowl. With a sigh, he took Stanley's spoon, searching through the milk for other Trix. "I already thought of that, Dad," Stanley put in. "You're thinking that the reds aren't the last ones to be eaten, but only the last to be floating, right? But like you can see, none of them sunk, either."

Stanley's dad put the spoon down, rubbed his face again, then winked. "But were they red to begin with?"

"What?"

"Maybe the last ones left are always red because after a certain amount of time exposed to milk, they all turn red." Stanley stared at the surviving Trix. His dad was right! How could he be certain that the three red Trix had started off being red? And what could he do about it? Stanley stared at the bowl, pondering the question. There just had to be a solution!

By the time Stanley looked up again, his dad was gone. His mom and Jerry weren't anywhere to be found either, which was just as well, because Stanley had finally figured out how to color test the Trix in milk. He grabbed five bowls from the cupboard, the box of Trix, and a gallon of milk, then hurried to his room. The entire box of Trix got dumped out on his bed, then divided into colors, one color for each bowl. Once each bowl was half full, he carried them all to his desk and poured in the milk. Stanley got out a role of white tape and wrote the original Trix color in each bowl on a piece of tape, sticking the tape to the corresponding bowl. Now all he had to do was wait.

Stanley flipped on the TV. Perfect! His favorite TV show, *Cowboy Roundup*, was just starting. He could check on the Trix during commercials. As far as Stanley knew, he was the only kid in his class who watched *Cowboy Roundup*. He'd even sent away for the *Cowboy Roundup Songbook*. That's mostly what *Cowboy Roundup* was—real-life cowboys singing cowboy songs and playing their instruments.

"Somebody shoot those guys!" Jerry said as he came into the room, using both hands to hold up a large bucket. "Oh, excuse me, somebody already did." Stanley did his best to ignore his brother's laughter, only that wasn't so easy, as Jerry spilled about half of whatever was in the bucket onto Stanley's back as he lifted it over him.

"Hey!" Stanley shouted, jumping up just in time to watch his brother climb onto his bed and dump the contents of the bucket into the fish tank. "What are you doing?" Stanley watched as a big, ugly gray fish swooshed into the tank, scattering the colored tropical fish that it had taken about three years to save up for. "You can't do that!"

Jerry just smiled. "Can't do it? Looks like I can, squirt. Can and did."

"But . . . but . . . but . . . what is that?" All the colored fish were hiding near the bottom, leaving the foot-long gray monster floating near the top, casually moving in and out of the strands of fake seaweed.

"Isn't it totally cool?" Jerry said, staring at the fish. "It's a trout. Alvin caught it this morning and traded it to me."

"Traded it?" Stanley scrunched up his face. "For what?"

That was when Jerry grabbed the little net that hung beside the tank and began to chase fish around the tank with it. "Half of the fish, of course."

"No!" Stanley yelled. "Leave my fish alone!" He tried to pull Jerry's arm out of the tank, only Jerry punched him in the ear, knocking him onto the rug.

"Half the fish are mine," Jerry said. "And so's half the tank. Just make sure your fish stay out of my fish's half, okay?" He scooped up fish after fish, dumping them into the bucket. Then he hurried out again.

After Jerry had slammed out the front door, Stanley put his head up against the fish tank, trying to count how many were left, only they were all hiding in the sunken ships and treasure chests that lined the bottom. Behind him a cowboy told a story of "the big Pecos River flood," how he and his friends had risked their lives to save all the cattle and even a goat or two. Stanley wondered if they'd be any good at saving tropical fish.

The first survivor to be spotted was the Yellow-Striped fish. Then the Blue-Striped fish. At last he saw his very favorite fish, the neon Glow-in-the-Dark fish. Stanley jumped into the air, shouting, "Yes, yes, yes!" and pumping his fist. The Glow-in-the-Dark fish was like a night-light that swam. It was also his greatest ally in the fight against aliens, vampires, and the like—when it moved nice and slow, the room was safe. However, if it ever sped up, that was a clear warning that some nonhumanoid, bloodsucking fiend was in the room and Stanley had better take immediate refuge in the laundry hamper.

Stanley watched the fish tank for ten more minutes, but nothing happened. His fish all stayed hidden on the bottom, while Jerry's trout swam aimlessly in circles near the top, so he went back to watching *Cowboy Roundup* and doing his extra-credit homework. After *Cowboy Roundup* a cowboy movie came on, and even though Stanley had seen it before, it was one of his favorites, so he watched it again. It wasn't until the movie was nearly over that he thought of the fish again, and that was only because Jerry came in again and said, "Hey, numbnuts, where'd your fish go?"

Stanley jumped to his feet, spinning toward the fish tank, and sure enough, the trout was now at the bottom and his fish were nowhere to be seen. He searched frantically, pulling on the cords to the sunken ships, waving the fish scoop through the fake seaweed. They just weren't there. "It ate them!" he screamed. "Your stupid trout ate all my fish!"

Jerry shrugged as he slipped out of one shirt, tossing it into a corner, and pulled a clean shirt out of his dresser. "It's a tough world, isn't it?" He pulled the shirt over his head and headed for the door. "But, hey, that's no reason to be a weenie about it."

Stanley continued to watch the trout swim around, hoping and praying that maybe some of his fish would pop out of the bigger fish's mouth, like Pinocchio and the whale. "Please," he asked, staring as the trout moved from one end of the tank to the other. "Just give me back my Glow-in-the-Dark fish. You can have the rest. You'll want to have someone to play with, anyway, and Jerry won't ever get anyone for you. I swear, he never will, no matter what he told you. Please? I'll even feed you extra hot dogs or anything you want. Okay?"

But instead of letting the Glow-in-the-Dark fish go, all the stupid trout did was float to the top and die.

the zoo

"It died?" Jerry's puzzled face blossomed into a huge grin. "Cool! I'll get Alvin. He's got some dissecting equipment."

"You're going to cut it up?"

"Sure! Don't you want to know if it ate all your weenie fish whole or if it took all sorts of bites? Who knows, maybe we can even sew them back together. Frankenfish!" Jerry was already out the door, not waiting for an answer.

Stanley sighed, staring at the dead trout. If he stayed around, Jerry and Alvin would probably tie him up and make him watch. He sighed again, then turned and followed his brother out of the house. Maybe, Stanley hoped, maybe Jerry and Alvin would bury his fish. Maybe they would even make a little cross and remember the names of all his fish, and even write them down on a little plaque. Stanley kicked at the ground as he walked. *Fat chance,* he thought. More likely, they would just dump them in the toilet, then bet on which one was the last to circle down into the drain.

Outside, Stanley turned away from the Lanorsky house. He walked with his head down, wondering what he would do with the rest of his life. Robby would probably never talk to him again, George and Jimmy didn't much like him to begin with, and Uncle Willie, the only person he'd ever known who'd undergone a successful personality transplant, couldn't even give him a clue as to how he'd done it. And now his Glow-in-the-Dark fish was gone, leaving him with no alien early-warning system, which meant that he'd probably have to sleep in the laundry hamper for the rest of his life. Sooner or later, his mom would notice that he'd taken on a permanent odor of Jerry's gym socks, and then what would he do?

Stanley realized that he'd walked onto his Rock-Kicking course, but he made no effort to find any rocks. He didn't look around for the ESPN van either. It was only a matter of time, after all, before they dropped him too. Instead of Stanley Krakow, Boy Wonder, they'd be calling him Smelly Socks Stanley. Or maybe Funky Foot Krakow. Stanley sighed again, kicking at a clump of grass. His whole life was useless. Totally useless!

Without thinking about it, he found himself standing in front of the hedge that surrounded Theresa Wasnicki's house. Stanley listened for voices, even for the sound of scissors, but except for the drone of a television inside the house, the air was quiet. Maybe she was in her yard again, crying. Maybe Stanley could help her. He kicked at the clump of grass again. How could he help anyone when he couldn't even help himself?

"Hey!" he heard a familiar voice shout. "Watch out!" Robby landed on Stanley's shoulders, laughing. "How's the human brain?" Robby asked. "Hey," he said again, dropping to the ground, "I've been calling you all morning. You know your phone's off the hook?" All Stanley could do was shrug. "Want to go to the zoo this afternoon? We're taking the bus. First, though, I have to drop off this invitation to my birthday party. You know my mom—she says it'd be rude not to invite the new kid. You know her name?"

"Theresa with an 'h,' Wasnicki with an 's,'" Stanley said automatically.

"Cool," Robby said. "The brain delivers again! Can I borrow your pen?" Stanley pulled a red pen out of his pocket, letting his friend use his back to jot down the name on the front of the invitation. Robby tucked in his shirt, then pulled Stanley with him toward the gate. "Come on, we'll invite her together! Man, Stan, I'm glad you were around!"

They pulled open a squeaky metal gate, then walked up a winding front walk and up three steps to the front porch. Without hesitating, Robby knocked on the door, loud and clear. Stanley stepped to the side, just in case a dog rocketed out when it opened. A kid could never be too careful. Only the door didn't open. Robby rang the bell, then knocked again, louder this time. "Well, that's that," he said with a shrug. "I tried."

He was just stuffing the invitation into the screen when the door was suddenly pulled open. A large woman glared down at them. "I suppose you're the neighborhood hooligans, banging on the door like that?"

Robby turned to Stanley. "Hooligans?" Stanley bent to his ear, whispering. "Oh, hooligans!" He turned back to the woman, grinning. "No, ma'am, we're not hooligans. You must be thinking of our older brothers, Charles and Jerold. We're the good brothers, Robert and Stanley. We came to deliver—" Without waiting for another word, the door slammed shut in his face. ". . . this invitation to my birthday party," Robby finished, holding out the card to the closed door. "Wow," he said to Stanley, "I'm somehow thinking they don't get invited to many parties." He left the invitation leaning against the door, then hopped down the steps. "Come on, Stan, we're meeting George and Jimmy at my house in . . ." He glanced at his watch. "Two minutes ago."

Robby set off at a run for his house, Stanley puffing to keep up. It was no act either—Stanley was always amazed at how his body seemed to instantly know whether he should be the Very Famous Stanley Krakow, Superathlete, or the Subzero Wimpoid Loser Stanley. He must have a computer for a mind. Someday they would write books about it.

Just as they reached Robby's front lawn Mrs. Lanorsky opened the door. "Are you boys ready?" she called. "Hop in the car. I have to hurry."

"Mom," Robby said, "a few changes in your plans. First of all, we're not little kids—we can take the bus, okay? Second, we have to wait for George and Jimmy."

"George and Jimmy aren't coming," Mrs. Lanorsky

told them. "They called and said George's dad was taking them bowling."

"And they didn't even invite us? The jerks!" Robby said with a snarl.

"Robert Henry, that is no way to talk about people. And it wasn't George's fault—George's dad said only one guest. And, after all, you weren't here."

"They could have at least waited until I got back," Robby complained, pouting.

Stanley turned away, embarrassed by the smile on his face. George and Jimmy weren't coming! He hardly ever got to go anywhere alone with Robby. "Well, their loss," Robby finally said. "Anyway, we're taking the bus. We're not kids, you know."

"Robert, I've said this before: The bus doesn't go to the zoo from here. It goes downtown, and downtown is full of men who drink too much liquor and who knows what else."

"Winos, Mom. Just call them winos, like everyone else does," Robby informed her. "Besides, we transfer to the zoo bus."

"And what if you forget to transfer? What then?" When Robby didn't answer, Mrs. Lanorsky sighed. "I'd worry all day, thinking that you might be downtown with the . . . with the winos."

"Ahem," Stanley said, hoping he'd be noticed.

"What is it, Stanley?" Mrs. Lanorsky asked pleasantly.

"Well, you see . . ." He gulped a big breath and took out his bus map, which he just happened to have in his shirt pocket, always prepared for any immediate getaway that might be required from space aliens or monsters. "You see, Mrs. Lanorsky, even if we miss the zoo bus, we can get on the number nine and then the number four. See? That gets us to the zoo too." She still looked doubtful. "They give you a new transfer every time you change buses. You can ride forever."

Robby grabbed the map. "No fooling?" he asked. So Stanley showed them, using his red ballpoint pen to circle each connection point. "And they really give you transfers every time?" When Stanley nodded, Robby began to laugh, like that was the best joke he'd ever heard. Even his mom began to laugh a little "Zamborific!" he said, slapping Stanley on the back. "Totally, absolutely, and fantastically Zamborific! Man, Stan, you must be the smartest kid around! Wow, you might even be the smartest kid on Earth! Think of it, Mom, I might know the smartest kid on Earth!"

Stanley blushed and smiled, and Mrs. Lanorsky said, "Well, as long as you're taking the smartest kid on Earth with you, Robert . . . and," she added without smiling, "as long as you follow his advice . . . you can take the bus."

"Victory!" Robby shouted. "I mean," he added

quickly, smiling at his mother, "we'll be very careful." He ran into his house, snatched a couple of gum balls from the candy tray by the front door, then raced back outside and grabbed Stanley.

The bus stop for the number one was only a block away, so they ran the whole way, arriving a minute before the bus did. "Transfer, please," Robby said, hopping up the steps.

It may have been true that Stanley knew the transfer points for each and every bus in the city and where each transfer point led to, but when it came to actually asking for one, his mouth seemed to freeze. His mom was always telling him that he had to learn to speak up. "No one is going to laugh at you!" she always told him. "There is nothing to be afraid of!" Except that people *did* laugh at him and he *was* afraid. Minor details to his mother, Stanley supposed.

"I . . . I . . . I . . . ," he said to the bus driver, who had only just begun to notice that there was still someone waiting. "I need . . ."

"A transfer," Robby added smoothly, holding out a hand for the second ticket. "You know what my friend, the brain, here says?" he said as the bus driver tore off another transfer. "He says you can ride the bus forever if you only know the right places to transfer. Did you know that?"

The bus driver smiled, his eyebrows raising. "No fooling?" he said. "Learn something new every day."

The bus stayed nearly deserted the whole way to the transfer point, and the bus to the zoo wasn't crowded either, so they got to roll the gum balls up and down the aisle, racing them when the bus stopped and started. Stanley had, of course, chosen the red one, leaving Robby with the blue—it was almost cheating, because the red won almost every time.

At the zoo entrance the boys leaped down the bus stairs, Robby laughing as the bus driver yelled for them to stop running. Stanley would have loved to stop running, only his friend was already racing through the "twelve-and-under" turnstile. The gate attendant opened his window, yelling at Robby's back, "You little twerp, where's your twelve-and-under card?" Of course, Robby didn't stop, which meant that Stanley had to run through also. Those were the rules. He felt the attendant's hand graze his shirt as he passed, reaching for him. But then he was by. Robby stuck a fist into the air. "Yes!" he said. "I knew you wouldn't wimp out."

They walked quickly past the flamingo pond, past Bear Drive and Antelope Lane, straight to The World's Biggest Reptile House, which had about every type of killer snake ever invented. Of course, they had every other type of snake too, but the dangerous ones all had red "poisonous" circles next to their names, or yellow "hazardous" circles, which made it easy for Robby and Stanley to run past the crowds surrounding the many snakes that could cause no harm.

Robby and Stanley got right to work, stopping first at the African tricolored cobra. DEATH IN THIRTY SECONDS, the sign read. NO KNOWN ANTIDOTE. "I nominate Steve Klemp," Robby said. He kept his eyes on the snake, but even then, Stanley could see him imagining what would happen to the bully who lived down the street from them. His skin would turn blue, then red, then yellow, just like the colors of the snake. All the while, he would be screaming for help, but Stanley knew Robby wouldn't lift a finger. Neither would he. After all, they had only thirty seconds to watch, and thirty seconds wasn't much when you considered all the time Steve Klemp had spent chasing them around the neighborhood, yelling about how he was going to beat them to a bloody pulp. "Well?" Robby asked.

For a moment Stanley didn't answer. It was a horrible way to die, tricolored skin poisoning, even if Steve Klemp liked to beat everyone up. He hadn't actually beaten up Stanley, or Robby, for that matter, but that might just be because he hadn't caught them yet. He was always talking about how many kids he clobbered on the way to school and how many he was planning to clobber on the way home from school and how his dad went to a bar last night and clobbered just about everyone who was there. So, to be on the safe side, Stanley said, "Okay. Death in thirty seconds for Steve Klemp."

Next, they came to the South American green tree snake: SEVERE RASH, ITCHING, AND PUSTULES. LASTS UP TO TWO WEEKS.

"What're pustules?" Robby asked.

"Like zits."

"Zits?" Robby smiled mischievously. "Who hates zits? I mean, who'd rather die than have zits?"

"Charles?"

"Yes! I nominate my repulso brother Charles for the green tree snake!"

Charles spent practically every waking minute in the bathroom, combing his hair, checking for the first signs of a mustache, and generally thinking that every girl in the neighborhood was in love with him. Fat chance! The worst part was, if Stanley had to use the bathroom over at the Lanorskys' house, Charles wouldn't leave. "Come right on in," Charles would say. *"Mi casa es su casa,"* or something just as dumb. Then he'd look in the mirror, making sure Stanley knew that he was watching, and say stupid things like, "Just go with the flow, little bro. Don't mind me." Like anyone could actually do anything with him staring in the mirror!

"Excellent choice," Stanley said. "Agreed."

"George and Jimmy get the horned viper," Robby then announced.

"The horned viper?" Stanley said. "Death within hours? Vomiting and convulsions?"

Robby nodded firmly. "That'll teach them to go bowling without us, won't it?"

Stanley looked away from the glass case enclosing the viper, hoping Robby wouldn't notice. He had actually been glad they went bowling. "Will you give them the antidote?" he asked, hesitantly.

Robby shrugged. "I don't know. What do you think?"

"Well, George did teach us about crawdads."

"But he didn't really know anything."

"But he tried. And he did fall in and get muck all over him."

Robby smiled, then began laughing. "That was good, all right. Yes, that was definitely worth the price of admission." Then his mean face came back. "What about Jimmy? Jimmy never taught us anything."

"Jimmy gave us snow cones last week."

"His mom gave us snow cones," Robby corrected.

"Sure, but she wouldn't have given them to us if we didn't know Jimmy or if Jimmy was . . . dead. Especially if she found out that it was us who killed him."

Robby nodded, thinking. "Okay," he said at last. "Fair's fair, after all. We give 'em the antidote. But only after they puke their guts out. Deal?"

"Deal," Stanley agreed. The two boys gave each other their secret handshake, the one Robby said came from the lost world of Zambor, pinkie fingers linked together, knocking elbows twice. Only on the lost world of Zambor the natives had three arms with two hands each, which made it a lot more interesting.

the return of alvin bagley's trout

The first thing Stanley heard as he came into the house was his mom screaming. No doubt about it, his talent was expanding—now he was coming home at the wrong time even on weekends. "Stanley!" she shouted from his bedroom. "Get in here! And don't even pretend that you can't hear me," she added as Stanley turned back toward the door.

Stanley came into his room to find his mom spraying a bottle of Windex at a trail of ants winding its way from the windowsill to the five bowls of soggy Trix he'd forgotten from the morning. "Oops," he said.

"See, Mom, it was a scientific experiment, see? Actually, it was Dad's idea."

"I don't care whose idea it was, just take the bowls into the kitchen. And don't spill anything on the floor!" she added as he lifted two bowls. The sound of her voice nearly knocked both bowls to the ground, but Stanley hung on. He walked carefully, spilling nothing. On his way he noticed that every bowl, no matter what the label said, was now filled with Trix the color of paste. And black spots. However, on closer examination the black spots turned out to be dead ants floating in the milk. At least he could tell his dad that the Trix didn't turn red.

After the mess was cleaned up and his mom had left his room, Stanley got out his newest library book, *The Life and Times of Jackie Robinson*, then lay on his bed to read. Only the light was dimmer than usual. It was the fish tank, Stanley noticed when he started looking around—its light had been turned off. Stanley jumped up, reaching over to the on/off switch, and flipped on the light. And screamed.

"If it's more ants," his mom called from another room, "get the Windex and clean them up yourself!"

But it wasn't ants. It was worse, far, far worse. Gently bobbing in the curls of fake seaweed and staring directly into Stanley's eyes was a large fish skeleton.

It seemed to be smiling. Other, smaller fish skeletons were inside it, all bobbing with the flow of the filter.

Stanley grabbed his book and ran outside, ducking under the house and into his secret hideout. Even then, he had trouble not hyperventilating. How was he ever going to get to sleep with a bunch of fish skeletons staring at him?

At dinner, unfortunately, they had fish. Stanley thought he might throw up. The only thing that saved him was that it didn't have any bones in it, but then he realized that the bones might not be on his plate only because Jerry had somehow gotten ahold of them.

"How was the zoo?" his mom asked.

Stanley's face turned red remembering how after he and Robby had gone through the World's Biggest Reptile House, they'd been thrown out of the zoo gift shop. It wasn't their fault, it was just that they didn't have any money left and they wanted to play with the plastic snakes. Stanley had been telling Robby about Poombah sticks when the manager, Mr. Grumpface, started yelling at them, saying that they were trying to steal his merchandise. Somehow Stanley didn't think his mom would want to hear about that, so he just mumbled, "Great." Then, to change the subject, he added, "Can I have another Glow-in-the-Dark fish?"

"Why would you want any more fish?" his dad asked. "Don't you have enough already?"

Jerry kept his face down, shoveling mashed potatoes into his mouth, but Stanley could see him rolling his eyes. "They all got eaten," Stanley said.

His dad looked up, staring crossly at Jerry. "Eaten? How'd they get eaten?"

"Well," Jerry said, swallowing a huge mouthful of potatoes, "remember last Saturday night, when you went out and told me to fix dinner? Only we were out of bologna for the bologna cups? Who'd believe it, but those little fish curl up even better! Great with cheese too."

"Jerry!" their mom shouted.

"Hey, I'm only kidding," he said quickly when no one laughed. "It was just one of those things—you know, law of the jungle, big fish eats little fish."

"They weren't in the jungle, Jerry," his dad said sternly. "They were in a fish tank."

Jerry rolled his eyes again. Their dad licked his fork clean of potatoes and pointed it in Jerry's direction, about to launch into a lecture, only Stanley cut him off. "Who cares where they were?" he practically shouted. "If I don't get another Glow-in-the-Dark fish, I'm going to smell like Jerry's gym socks for the rest of my life!"

His dad stared at Stanley for a moment. No one spoke. "Did I miss something?" he finally said. When the silence continued, he added, "Of course you can have more fish. Just save your allowance."

"But that'll take months!" Stanley said.

"Money doesn't grow on trees," his dad told him, returning his attention to his fork. "If it did, I'd be in the forestry business." His dad laughed heartily at his own joke, not seeming to notice that no one else was laughing with him. "The fish is great, honey." He smiled, digging in. "Thanks for de-boning it."

Stanley watched his mom poking at her fish with a fork, her face puckering. "That's odd," she murmured, "I don't remember de-boning it."

sweet dreams

As soon as the lights went off that evening, Stanley knew he was in trouble. Big trouble. The fish skeletons floated in the darkness above his head, glowing white, staring down at him. Stanley stared back, afraid to close his eyes. Were they all turned in his direction? Watching him? Even though it wasn't very cold, Stanley pulled his blanket up tighter around him, covering as much skin as possible—after all, it didn't take a genius to figure out what a skeleton most wanted in the world. Then he had another horrible thought: Fish had to stay in the tank, but what about fish skeletons? They didn't actually breathe, did they?

That was when the skeletons jumped. "Eeek!" Stanley peeped. He must be imagining things. "I must be," he said out loud. "I must be, I must be!" Then he saw the skeletons jump again, clawing at the side of the tank, trying to rise up. Stanley leaped out of his bed, tearing for the bathroom. Behind him he heard Jerry tittering, but even then, he didn't stop. Maybe it was a joke and maybe it wasn't; Stanley certainly wasn't going to stick around to find out.

The next morning Stanley awoke early, absolutely determined to earn enough money by the end of the day to buy another Glow-in-the-Dark fish. He didn't care what he had to do, nothing could be worse than dreaming of flesh-eating skeleton fish searching the house for him—if he actually had been dreaming. He started with his regular chores, which he had to get done before he could have his allowance. Jerry was still asleep, so Stanley worked quietly, making his bed, dusting the shelves, cleaning the top of the dresser. That was when he discovered the clear plastic thread tied to the fish skeletons, rising out of the side of the tank nearest to Stanley's bed, then dropping down the dresser, running under it to Jerry's bed. *Very funny,* Stanley thought.

Luckily, one of Stanley's chores was cleaning the

fish tank, something he usually hated to do. Not today, though. Today he would have done it for free. He got a trash bag from the kitchen, then, standing on his bed, he pulled the skeleton fish up by the plastic thread, depositing them into the bag. And he didn't just dump the bag in the trash cans at the side of the house either. No, that would have been too easy. That would have been something Jerry might have planned on. Instead, Stanley walked five blocks to an out-of-the-way Dumpster. Even then, he made sure the fish skeletons were buried beneath a load of other trash.

For the rest of the day Stanley worked around the house, polishing furniture, sweeping the sidewalks, washing his mom's car. He even washed his dad's car after he got home that afternoon. Still, when he sat down to count his money at the kitchen table, he was three dollars short of even the cheapest Glow-in-the-Dark fish. "It's not fair!" he whined.

Jerry sat down at the table next to Stanley, a bologna-cup sandwich on his plate. "Too bad you dumped the skeletons for free," he taunted. "I would have paid you. Hey! I have an idea," he said, taking a huge bite of bologna and egg yolk. "How about I pay you to bring them back?"

"Jerry," their mom warned, "don't tease your brother. And especially not with your mouth full."

"Just kidding," he said, taking another bite. "But really, how about I help pay for the fish? We can pick it out tonight."

Stanley's mouth dropped open. "For real?" he asked.

Jerry nodded, finishing his sandwich with the next bite. "Sure," he mumbled through a full mouth of food. "After all, it was my fish that ate your fish. One condition, though: I get to pick out the fish."

"But it'll be a Glow-in-the-Dark fish?"

"Scout's honor," Jerry said, smiling brightly. "In fact, I'll buy you two of them."

Stanley frowned. Jerry had never been a Scout. On the other hand, he couldn't just be lying, not with his mom right there. Could he?

To Stanley's surprise, Jerry didn't even fix himself another sandwich, but went right to his room to get his wallet. Fifteen minutes later they were at the fish store.

"My," their mom said, "these really *are* expensive." Stanley and his mom wandered up and down the aisles, Stanley pointing out the different fish that glowed in the dark. "Why aren't any of them glowing now?" his mom asked.

Stanley sometimes wondered if there shouldn't be a test or something that you had to take before you got to be an adult—they seemed to not know the simplest things. "They glow in the dark, Mom," he told her. "It's not dark in here."

"Oh."

Jerry rushed up one of the aisles, a large, clear plastic bag in his hands. "Got 'em!" he said. Inside the bag two rather plain-looking fish darted from side to side. "Special deal, the second one's only half price."

Stanley stared at the fish, frowning. "You're sure they're Glow-in-the-Dark fish?"

Jerry beamed. "Oh boy, am I sure!" It was all he could do to not start laughing. Stanley's frown grew deeper—anything that made Jerry so happy couldn't possibly be a good thing. "You don't believe me?" Jerry asked innocently. "Let's go into the darkroom and check them out."

There was a small room in the back used to illuminate phosphorescent fish, lit only with purple bulbs. It also lit up your smile if you used the right kind of toothpaste, but their dad would never buy it. "You can buy new teeth for less than that stuff costs," their dad had told them when they'd asked.

"Go on," their mom said to Stanley when he hesitated. "Go with your brother."

"Ready?" Jerry asked when Stanley finally got back to the tiny room.

Stanley hesitated in the open doorway, not at all sure that he was ready. Once he closed the door, the room would be completely dark.

"Hey!" Jerry barked. "You want the fish or not?"

"I guess," Stanley answered. Slowly, he stepped forward, pulling the door closed.

Immediately, the dim figure of his brother holding the fish in a bag disappeared. Stanley held his breath, forcing himself not to bolt out the door—he had wisely kept hold of the doorknob. Then, slowly, the glow of something all too familiar began to take shape. Two white, bony spines appeared, floating disconnected at the end of Jerry's arm. Next, two white, bony heads appeared, along with white bony rib cages. "Skeleton fish," Jerry said proudly. "Glow-in-the-Dark Skeleton fish!" And even without the special toothpaste, Stanley could see his brother smiling.

mr. grumpface

Actually, the fish weren't so bad, Stanley thought as he lay in bed that evening, watching them move slowly back and forth in their new home. After all, they *did* glow. And who could tell, they might even scare away some of the lesser creatures of the night. At the very worst any night creature looking in would see that they weren't very well fed in this house and go looking for plumper prey.

As Stanley walked to school the next day he thought about how great it was to start the week not smelling like Jerry's gym socks. Plus, he didn't even come close to being called on during reading-aloud period that Monday, and because school ended in another week, everyone ran around and got into trouble, and Mrs. Olsen hardly noticed Stanley setting holding-your-breath records. He had to go to the principal's office only once all week, and that was only because Steve Klemp put glue in his hair during art period, when he was drawing a very complicated map of the lost world of Zambor, and it dried into a huge spike. To make the week almost perfect, Jimmy and George got into so much trouble that their parents put them on restriction, and they couldn't go to the zoo on Saturday with Robby.

"Now, remember," Mrs. Lanorsky began as they set off to the zoo.

"Mom, we remember, we remember!" Robby interrupted. "How can we forget? One, pay attention to the bus driver. Two, always keep a quarter in case we have to make an emergency call. And three"—he smiled, winking at Stanley—"always have a plan of attack."

"What was that?" his mom asked.

"A plan for a snack," Robby said innocently. He reached into the candy tray, grabbing a handful of gum balls. "Don't want to get hungry. Come on," he said to Stanley, "I'll race you to the bus stop."

Robby didn't have to worry about beating Stanley;

he could beat Stanley running backward. He could beat George and Jimmy, too, but he had to run forward. Only today it didn't matter how fast he ran—someone was there before him.

"What's the rush?" Theresa Wasnicki said as Robby ran up, Stanley puffing behind him. She was leaning on the bus stop signpost, arms and legs crossed, like maybe she owned the place. Up close her eyes were so black that they sparkled. Stanley smiled shyly when she looked at him, then lowered his head.

"Revenge," Robby whispered in a low voice.

"Revenge?" Stanley said. He thought they were just going to the zoo.

"Revenge." Theresa worked the word around in her mouth a bit, then smiled. "Interesting. And just who are you revenging?"

Just then the bus arrived, the doors swinging open. Robby jumped on. "We'll tell you all about it when we get back. *If* we get back," he added, climbing the steps.

Stanley followed, though he wasn't at all sure he wanted to. When they'd gotten thrown out of the zoo gift shop the week before, Robby had said that he'd get even. But Robby was always saying stuff like that, so Stanley hadn't thought much about it. Now he wished that George and Jimmy hadn't been put on restriction. Or maybe that he'd been put on restriction with them.

It wasn't until he sat down next to Robby that he noticed Theresa right behind him.

"You look like you'll need some help," was all she said.

"But . . ." Stanley remembered Theresa's mom. "Don't you need to ask permission?" he said.

"I guess I'm old enough to do what I want," Theresa answered, then settled back in the seat opposite Robby and Stanley, arms folded across her chest, scowling at them. A few seconds later, though, she sighed, her face softening. "Actually, my parents left yesterday, if you want to know the truth. And they probably won't be back until tomorrow. I'm supposed to stay at home, but . . ." Theresa shrugged. "It's boring. So if that's a problem . . ."

Robby just grinned. "The more the merrier," he said.

Stanley had a big problem with that, only he said nothing. Actually, he had a lot of big problems. What if Robby got caught? Summer vacation was coming. What if Robby got put on restriction until school started again? Who would Stanley play with then? Forget about George and Jimmy—the only reason they even talked to Stanley was because Robby made them. What if every single day of summer his mom sent him out to play with his friends, only there weren't any? And what about Theresa's mom? Stanley could just imagine her knocking on their front door, demanding to see the person who'd gotten her daughter arrested.

Robby filled Theresa in on how Mr. Grumpface, the manager of the zoo gift shop, had thrown them out the week before. "He said we were trying to steal the snakes! We weren't trying to steal them, we were just playing with them! Why would anyone throw a snake up in the air for everyone to see if he was planning to steal it?"

"So what's the plan?" Theresa asked. Robby opened his mouth to speak, then closed it again. Theresa shook her head. "I waste a whole quarter on the bus, and you don't even have a plan? Typical boys," she huffed. "No plan, not even a clue."

For the first time ever Stanley saw Robby blushing. "Stan's the brain," he said lamely. "You have a plan, right, Stan? . . . Right?" he said again when Stanley didn't answer. "After all, he kicked you out too."

For a while Stanley stared at his hands. "He's thinking," Robby told Theresa in a hopeful voice. "He's definitely thinking."

After a few minutes Stanley looked up, smiling timidly. "What?" Robby asked. "Come on, tell!"

Stanley's voice was low, and he didn't look at them

when he spoke. Even then, it was hard for him to find the right words, and if Robby and Theresa hadn't kept saying, "Good, good, what next?" he probably wouldn't have been able to finish. Only he did finish.

For a moment no one said anything, and Stanley thought that maybe he'd only imagined telling them his plan. But then Robby shouted, "Stan, you're a genius. A genius!"

"Wow," Theresa said as they walked in the zoo entrance. Before her was the flamingo pond—over fifty pink flamingos and every one of them standing on just one leg, the other pulled up beneath them. "How do they do that?"

"That?" Robby said. "That's nothing. Wait until you see the bears! And the tigers! And the elephants! Come on, Stan, let's give her the two-hour tour!"

The two-hour tour consisted of running from exhibit to exhibit, yelling, "Gangway! Coming through! Where's the rest rooms?" at each turn, and generally cramming what took most people eight hours to do into one fourth of the time. "After all," Robby said, "it's the least we can do for you before we . . . before we . . ."

"Before we die," Stanley finished for him.

"Exactly," Robby said. And off they went, touring

Bear Drive, Lion Alley, and the World's Biggest Reptile House, not slowing until they ended up at the birdhouse exhibit.

The birdhouse was actually a huge, football field–size cage, so totally massive that it had its own stream running through it, from top to bottom, with a winding path running next to it and a sign that warned people to stay on the path: THE BIRDS IN THIS DISPLAY MAY BE NESTING. PLEASE RESPECT THEIR NEED FOR PRIVACY.

"Right!" Robby said as he pushed inside the walk-in exhibit. "If the birds need privacy so much, whose great idea was it to stick them in a cage? Anyway, that's just for adults. Kids can go wherever they want."

"Just who told you that?" Theresa asked.

"A little birdie." Robby grinned. "Look, it's obvious—if they'd meant kids, they would've put up a fence instead of this bar that you can duck under." And to prove it, he swung under the bar. "See?" he said. "Come on, let's find some bird feathers!" Without waiting for an answer, he immediately disappeared into the bushes.

After ducking under the bar Stanley looked at the ground and frowned. If there were any feathers, he couldn't see them. He began moving closer to Robby. What if the birds didn't particularly like kids looking for their feathers? What if the birds were hungry? But all he said was, "You find any yet?"

"No." Robby stood up. "But I think someone's already been here. Look at this." Stanley looked at where Robby was pointing. Footsteps. Large ones. "See?" he said.

"You don't think someone's still in here, do you?" Stanley asked, staring over Robby's shoulder.

"You mean, like watching us?" Theresa asked. She moved closer, gazing around her.

"Like illegal bird hunters?"

"Or runaway prisoners?"

"Or cannibals?"

"Nah," Robby said, giving them his best smile. "No way." They all turned at the same instant, hollering incoherently as they scrambled back onto the path.

No one needed to say anything after that; they all knew what came next. They stopped at a refreshment stand, asking for empty cups. For water, they said. After that they walked silently toward the zoo gift shop.

Stanley went in first, followed by Theresa a minute later, and Robby last of all. They pretended to not know one another, drifting through the store, picking up objects, holding them up, putting them back. Mr.

Grumpface did his best to observe them all, but it was impossible. He hurried from one aisle to another, spurred on by their suspicious behavior, their backward glances at him, the way they moved to another aisle every time they noticed him watching.

When the gift shop clock clicked to two o'clock, they all wandered into aisle three. Theresa started laughing, but she stopped when Robby poked an elbow into her arm. Just as he had done the week before, Mr. Grumpface watched them from the next aisle over, staring through a display of carved elephants, tiny tusks poking into his chin. "Now!" Robby whispered. Each of them picked up a snake and dropped it into their water cups. Then they hurried for the door.

"Stop!" Mr. Grumpface shouted, but they were already outside. "Thieves!" he cried, racing after them. "Scoundrels!"

The three of them ran out the zoo exit and down the tree-lined street, toward the Museum of Natural History. Mr. Grumpface was close behind them, not gaining, but not falling behind, either. "Stop!" he yelled again, and to his utter amazement, Theresa did just that, so quickly that Mr. Grumpface nearly stumbled over her. He recovered quickly, one hand grabbing Theresa by the back of her shirt, the other grabbing the cup in her hand. "Ha!" he said. "I've got you now!" But all he found inside the cup was a big hole in the bottom. "What . . . what is this?" Robby and Stanley started to snicker.

"Holes," Robby explained. He was smiling triumphantly. "There's no law against not stealing stuff. Is there, Mr. Grumpface?"

"What . . . what did you call me? Mr. . . . Mr. what?" he bellowed.

"Grumpface," Robby said calmly. "That's what everybody calls you."

Mr. Grumpface let go of Theresa, who tumbled to the ground. "I hate kids!" he snarled, grabbing for Robby. "I hate them!" Robby ducked under Mr. Grumpface's hand, but then he tripped over Theresa, sprawling on the ground at Grumpface's feet. "Ha!" Grumpface said again. "Got you!"

Robby and Theresa tried to scoot backward, but there was no escape. Worse than that, far worse, a new menace came up behind Mr. Grumpface; Stanley was the only one who even saw it coming. Stanley wanted to yell to his friends to run, but it was already too late. His eyes clamped shut, he wondered what his mom would think about tomorrow's headlines: STANLEY AND FRIENDS ARRESTED; STANLEY AND FRIENDS SENT AWAY TO REFORM SCHOOL. But when he finally opened his eyes, he saw the strangest sight: The police-man who'd come up behind Mr. Grumpface was hold-ing one of the paper cups, poking his fingers through the cutout bottom. And smiling.

the new and improved stanley krakow!

"So what happened next?" Uncle Alan asked. The visitors' lounge was nearly empty, the sun just setting, and beyond the picture windows the city was turning into a blaze of orange. Stanley had begged his mom to take him to see Uncle Willie—he had to be careful with his mom to call him Uncle Willie and not Uncle Alan—but even then, she wouldn't come upstairs to visit. She said she would go shopping and pick him up in an hour.

"It was great, Uncle Alan! Mr. Grumpface wanted the policeman to arrest us for shoplifting. Only we didn't steal anything, on account of the snakes just fell through the bottoms of our cups, right back into the display. So Mr. Grumpface told the policeman to arrest us for pretending to steal the snakes! And you know what the policeman did?"

"No, what?" Uncle Alan waited for Stanley to speak. And for the first time in his life Stanley knew exactly what to say. He couldn't ever remember feeling better.

"He laughed! He said it was a very good joke!" Stanley started laughing just thinking about it. The policeman had looked at the holes in the cups and listened to Mr. Grumpface ordering him to arrest them, and he'd burst out laughing. Pretty soon Robby and Theresa began laughing, and then even Stanley was laughing.

"Then Grumpface totally lost it!" Stanley told his uncle. "'Whose side are you on?' he yelled at the policeman. 'I'm on the side of the law,' the policeman told him." Stanley deepened his voice to sound like the policeman. "'So if I see you manhandling any more children, I'll be forced to arrest you. Is that perfectly clear?' Mr. Grumpface just stood there." Stanley giggled. "And his mouth kept going up and down, but he couldn't say a word! And afterward Theresa and Robby congratulated me, on account of it was all my plan!"

Uncle Alan guffawed, patting Stanley on the back. "I'm glad you're my nephew, son. I sure wouldn't want you on the other side! Reminds me a bit of the time I was in jail down in Guatemala. They thought I had a million dollars hidden somewhere." He winked at Stanley. "I did, too." Then Uncle Alan told him the story of how he'd escaped from jail and how that million dollars was still hidden in a hole, just waiting for him to return. Of course, so was the captain of police!

When Uncle Alan had finished his story, he stared out the window, watching the last of the sunset. Slowly, his smile faded. "How come your mom didn't come up to visit?" he asked. Stanley didn't know what to answer. "That's okay, I guess I know," Uncle Alan finally said. "She doesn't much like the new me, does she?"

Stanley shrugged. He didn't want to tell Uncle Alan all the things his mom said, about how he was just taking a vacation from life and how he was breaking everyone's heart. Instead, he said, "Maybe if you just came over for dinner like you used to, maybe she'd get to like you again."

Uncle Alan ruffled Stanley's hair. "I would if I could, my young man. But, unfortunately, they won't let me out of here until I'm back to my old self. The thing is, I like my new self better." He shook his head.

"They might not keep me here much longer either. They might send me away to . . . another hospital."

"But . . . I could still visit, couldn't I?"

"Maybe," Uncle Alan said. It was completely dark outside now, and the visitors' room, except for the two of them, was deserted. "I hope you can still visit." He sighed, then glanced at his watch. "Anyway, it's time you went downstairs. Your mom's waiting."

Stanley didn't want to get up. He wanted to tell his uncle that he would visit no matter where he was sent. Only, if it was too far away or if they didn't let kids in, how could he? "I don't see why you can't just be Uncle Alan now," he said instead. "You're still the same person, really—aren't you?"

Uncle Alan grinned, his eyebrows fluttering up and down. He stood, hoisting Stanley up from his chair and walking with him toward the elevator. "That's the question, isn't it? So let me ask you a question, Mr. Stanley: Now that your friends all think you're wonderful, are you the same person? Now that you can come in here and tell your uncle stories of your own, don't you think of yourself in a different way? And here's another question: Did you mean to change? Or was it something that just sort of popped out of you? Like sometime this year you'll just pop out of your clothes—they won't fit anymore. Comfortable as they might have been, you'll need new clothes, bigger clothes. Maybe you're growing into a new Stanley. A bigger Stanley."

Stanley didn't answer. At school, when Mrs. Olsen asked a question, there was a right answer and a wrong one, and if Stanley didn't know the right answer, he could find it. But now he just didn't know. He really didn't. "Your mom wants an easy answer, Stanley," his uncle said. "I wish I could give it to her." He sighed, then pushed the elevator button. "Whoever I am," he said with a smile, "you're still my nephew." Stanley just shrugged.

"Oh." Uncle Alan grinned. "Shrinking on me, are you?" He bent suddenly, grabbing Stanley by the waist and swinging him in a circle.

"Hey!" Stanley shouted. "You'd better not . . . " But it was already too late—his uncle swung him up and into the air.

"Hey!" Stanley shouted again, but this time he was laughing. "Don't drop me!"

Stanley rose toward the ceiling, then fell perfectly into Uncle Alan's arms. But instead of putting Stanley down, Uncle Alan swept him in another quick circle, then tossed him into the air again, higher this time. "I hardly ever drop anyone!" he said. On the next toss Stanley could have actually touched the ceiling. "Of course, there's always a first time!" Uncle Alan laughed.

"Hey!"

After the fifth toss Stanley was hysterical. So was his uncle. As the elevator door opened they collapsed onto the floor, unable to stop giggling and snorting. They laughed even louder when they realized that Stanley's mom had ridden the elevator up and was staring at them openmouthed.

"Thank you, Willie," she said coldly. "Now I believe it's time to leave, Stanley—your name is still Stanley?" his mom asked snidely, pulling him onto the elevator.

18

reading-aloud period

Even if his mom had wanted to talk, which she didn't, Stanley wouldn't have had much to say on the car ride home. He never had much to say on Sunday evenings, for after Sunday evening all there was to think about was Monday morning, and Monday morning meant reading-aloud period.

The funny part of it was that, at home, Stanley could read perfectly, even out loud. But in school, with people watching, something happened. First, his hands began to shake, and then his voice started getting louder or softer all on its own. Pretty soon after that it was like he was standing in a tunnel—everything began to echo inside his head, until the words he was reading didn't even sound like words to him.

Last Friday, at the beginning of math period, Mrs. Olsen had stood up behind her desk and rapped her ruler three times on a thick pile of graded math papers—which made it sound like someone getting his bottom whacked—and said that they would have a special math class that day, on account of no one was paying proper attention anyway. "You may not realize it, class," Mrs. Olsen announced, "but the study of mathematics may someday save your life!" Then she read the class stories from the newspaper, like one about this guy in a tiny boat who needed to figure out the perfect angle to sail up these humongous waves and one about this mountain climber who got lost and had to calculate the direction home. She even read a story about a woman who came up with the perfect system for winning at cards. Of course, the woman had to go to jail and give all the money back, so maybe that one wasn't such a good story after all.

Stanley already knew that math could save his life—it was how he got out of reading-aloud period every Monday morning. And if that didn't save his life, what did? First, he made a chart of how many kids on average were absent from school each day and the probability of where they were likely to be sitting. That was what Mrs. Olsen called a "graph." Usually, Stanley would have turned it in for a ton of extra credit, only he thought that probably Mrs. Olsen wouldn't appreciate this particular graph, so he was careful to keep it hidden. Next, he timed each kid's reading speed, so he could give them a WPM score—words per minute. The last part of his scheme was that every Sunday evening he would read all the paragraphs that the class would be reading for Monday's reading-aloud period, and he matched them to the kids who would probably be reading them. So he used his chart and his graph to figure out how many kids would probably be sick, and where they would most likely be sitting, and how long the kids who would be in class would take to read their paragraphs. And that was it—Stanley would know if he'd have to read or not. And if he did, if it was even close, he would stay home sick.

Staying home sick was the easy part, on account of just thinking about reading aloud made Stanley's stomach start to turn over—just like the time his dad had taken the family ocean fishing. There were about twenty people on the boat, but they made Stanley stand at the very back, because he kept throwing up. His dad and Jerry and almost everyone on the boat was mad at him until the captain explained that he was the reason the fishing was so good. "Whatever the boy ate this morning," the captain said with a laugh, "the fish sure do like!"

And that was how Stanley got out of reading-aloud period. There were only two things wrong with his system. First of all, he could never tell anyone what a total genius he was, on account of if his mom or Mrs. Olsen ever found out about it and made him go to school on reading-aloud days, he'd probably have to kill himself. The second problem was that sometimes it didn't work.

On the last Monday morning of school Stanley, like everyone else in class, didn't sit down after the bell rang. The entire class ran around, yelling and laughing, playing tag and throwing spitballs. After all, it was the last Monday of school! Mrs. Olsen just stood behind her desk, watching and smiling. That was the first clue that something was wrong—Mrs. Olsen never smiled. Suddenly, her yardstick blurred against the blackboard, the sound cracking like thunder through the room, so loud that kids actually ducked to the floor. "Seats," was all she said. In five seconds everyone was seated and quiet.

"Perhaps you think classes have been cancelled for this week," she went on. "I assure you, they have not. Everything—I repeat, everything—will be exactly as it has always been!"

Stanley knew what was coming, but he couldn't believe it. It just wasn't right! There had to be a rule about it! But like most things in life, the really important rules never got written down. He hung his head, waiting helplessly. "Open your readers, class. We will now have reading-aloud period."

Still, there was a chance. Stanley had counted out the paragraphs the evening before because even though he was absolutely certain no normal teacher would ever have reading-aloud period on the last day of school he decided, in the end, that Mrs. Olsen just couldn't be *completely* trusted. It would be close, and normally, he would have stayed home sick. But every other class was having parties and going on field trips, and Stanley hadn't wanted to miss out. And the likelihood of her making them read seemed so slim. Wrong, wrong wrong! He wanted to pound his head against his desk, but instead, he counted out how many kids would read before him. The good part was that every single kid but Theresa Wasnicki was in class, and Theresa's absence wouldn't matter, since she read after him and not before. Normally, he would have gotten out his little pocket notebook and written a note to himself in red ink, a reminder to knock on her door after school. At the moment, though, all Stanley could do was stare at the paragraphs, then at the kids who'd be reading them. He sighed. It would be very, very close!

Of course, there was always his secret weapon, his last line of defense—Steve Klemp, the slowest, most terrible reader in the whole class. In fact, Steve Klemp might have been the slowest, most terrible reader in the whole world. Stanley wondered if they kept world records for stuff like that. If they did, he would have to nominate Steve Klemp. It was the least he could do for having someone so dense sitting in front of him. Once, when Stanley had made a mistake about how many kids would be ahead of him, Steve Klemp had taken up a whole ten minutes on his paragraph. And he still had three sentences to go when the bell rang! Stanley had almost felt sorry for him, only he'd been too busy hyperventilating.

"Steven Klemp!" Mrs. Olsen said only five minutes into reading-aloud period. "What are you doing? What is that in your hand?"

Steve Klemp smiled crookedly, holding up a lizard. "I named him Godzilla," he said. "Want me to pass him around the room?"

"Principal's office!" Mrs. Olsen said with a bark. She quickly wrote out a note. "Now!"

And just like that, Stanley's last line of defense disappeared. He prayed for a fire drill or a nuclear attack or even a surprise visit from the president of the United States. He prayed that he would miraculously turn invisible, like he did when he put on his Dark Man mask, and that Mrs. Olsen would skip right over him.

"Stanley Krakow," Mrs. Olsen called out. "Go ahead, Stanley, stand up and read." He could barely hear her over the pounding thud of his heart. "Stanley," she said again, "stop dallying!"

So he began.

Stanley had noticed that in times of crisis his body had devised a unique strategy of defense—it tried to kill itself before anyone else had the chance. First, his throat tightened, making his words squeak out and the breath squeak in. He heard the first bits of stifled laughter. Listening to Stanley embarrass himself during reading-aloud period was why half the class came to school each Monday. Next, his mouth went so completely dry that his squeaking words seemed to catch on his tongue and lips, breaking apart into odd rushes of gibberish. After that his hands began to shake, just a tremble at first, but growing with each mangled word.

Halfway through his paragraph, with his hands shaking so badly that the book's pages were actually jumping up and down and he couldn't see the words any longer, Stanley decided to go home. It didn't matter to him what happened—nothing could be worse

than standing there with everyone watching and tittering.

"Stanley!" Mrs. Olsen shouted as he slammed the
book onto his desk and ran for the door. "Come back
here this instant!" But he didn't. He heard her shoes
clacking behind him, chasing him down the aisle and
out the door. For a brief moment he saw the kids of his
class lining the windows, opening them to shout, "Go,
Stanley, go! Go, Stanley, go!" But he didn't care. He
ran past the jungle gym, past the swings, onto the
sandlot playing field, and right into the street without
even looking.

"Stanley!" he heard Mrs. Olsen scream, her voice
even louder than before. "Watch out!"

He heard the squeal of brakes, turned just in time
to see a car barreling down on him. Stanley tripped,
and for a moment, as he sailed through the air, he
thought of how beautiful the world must look to his
Glow-in-the-Dark fish, suspended in their tank,
watching Jerry and Stanley come and go, come and go,
while everything they would ever need in life was
already there. Then he came down, his head pounding
hard against the asphalt.

theresa's secret

For a while Stanley remembered nothing, not the ambulance, not Mrs. Olsen crying and praying over him, not the breathing machines at the hospital. He dreamed of long, fat snakes slithering and tangling just in front of him, so close that he was sure they must be coming out of his eyeballs. Occasionally, he would open his eyes to see a doctor or a nurse, but he couldn't hear what they were saying, and besides, they seemed less real and less fascinating than the snakes. He wanted to get up and look around for a Poombah stick, only he felt too dizzy. Once he thought he saw his mom and dad. His mom was crying and waving her arms around, his dad was trying to hold her. Then he passed out again and didn't wake up until the next morning.

At first he just looked at the blue sky coming through the strange windows. It was the light blue of early morning, the color Stanley liked best, for it meant that whatever evil had chased him through the night was now banished from the world. He was still dreaming, of course. He knew that as soon as he looked around the room and saw his dad sleeping in the bed next to him. The bed had metal rails around it, just like his, only it was a kid's bed and his dad was too big for it, so his legs dangled over the railing. "Dad," he said, then louder, "Dad!" because his dad never slept this late, and besides, it was perfectly all right to wake up your dad in a dream.

His dad sat up slowly, rubbing his face. Then he looked over at Stanley and smiled. "Thank God," he said. Then again, "Thank God," almost laughing. "You had us worried for a while."

"Why?"

"Well," he started. Then he rubbed his face again, only this time it was to hide the tears in his eyes—it was the same thing Stanley did whenever he started to cry. "You had a concussion. For a while the doctors weren't so sure you'd be all right. You even stopped breathing." His dad's voice was quivering; he gulped down a deep breath and smiled. "But you're okay," he added with another smile. "You're okay now."

Stanley was beginning to believe that he wasn't dreaming, but he still didn't understand. "How come you're in bed? Are you sick too?"

His dad laughed, a nice sound to Stanley's ears—his dad hardly ever laughed. Then he pulled himself out of the bed and moved to a chair. "I wanted to be here when you woke up. I thought you might be scared, waking up alone in a strange place."

"Are you going to stay?" Stanley's throat felt suddenly hot and scratchy, like something was trying to crawl out of it. "Something's wrong," he said, his hands clutching his neck.

"You're not supposed to talk, that's all." His dad stepped to the bed, patting Stanley's head. "They had to put tubes down your throat, to make sure you could breathe. Are you thirsty? Hungry?" Stanley nodded. "I'll be right back."

His dad returned in a few minutes. "Ice cream," he said, smiling and holding out a bowl. "Your favorite, chocolate! That's all they'll let you eat for now. You know how much they charged for just one scoop? Well," he said, shaking his head, "that's probably not so important. Especially considering what the rest of this is going to cost," he said, almost to himself. "No talking," he added when Stanley started to speak. He glanced at his watch. "I have to go now," he said. "I'm still the boss, you know. Besides, the doctor said you need to rest, stay quiet. No visitors until they're sure you're okay. But your mom will be here in a few hours, and if everything's still okay, you might get to go home with her then."

Stanley's dad bent down to kiss him, his rough cheek rubbing against Stanley's. He hadn't shaved yet. Then he was gone. "Bye," Stanley said to the door.

A few minutes later a nurse came in, but she didn't have much to say. She took his temperature and blood pressure and warned him that even though he was feeling better, he needed to stay in bed. Then she left, telling him that she'd be back in an hour.

For a while Stanley watched the TV, but all that was on were game shows, which he hated. Fortunately, he had stayed up way past his bedtime two nights before, watching old war movies while waiting for Jerry to sneak back into the house. Stanley closed his eyes, pretending he was a prisoner of war, just like in the movies, only they wouldn't give him any food until he told them where his buddies were, the ones who were going to blow up the airfield. It had been ten days since they'd last fed him; he was so weak that he could barely stand up. Suddenly, the door to his cell was thrown open, and a big, ugly man with a twisted, red scar on his cheek walked in, followed by two guards. The German commander.

"Get up!" the commander ordered. "What do you think this is, a hospital? Hah!" The two guards forced Stanley to stand up.

Stanley smiled grimly. *I don't know why he bothers,* Stanley thought. *He knows I won't talk.* Only today the commander had discovered that chocolate ice cream was his favorite food of all time, and the two guards brought in a huge bowl of chocolate chip, his favorite of favorites, setting the bowl just out of reach. They'd even brought extra spoons, with which they took small bites, licking the ice cream slowly as Stanley watched.

"Mmm!" they said—it was the one word in German that Stanley understood without help.

"Ve vill see if you vill talk now!" the German commander sneered.

"I'll never talk!" Stanley told him. "Never, you slimy crawdad!"

The commander continued to laugh, but something went out of his voice. Finally, he stopped altogether. "Vat is a crawdad?" he asked.

"Hah!" Stanley barked. The commander didn't

know when his men would attack, and he didn't know what a crawdad was. In Stanley's book that made him little more than pond scum.

"Enough!" the commander shouted. "You have five minutes. Only five minutes! Then the torture chamber! Go!" he said to his men. "Prepare it!"

With that, the commander and his guards swept out of the room, leaving Stanley to wonder exactly what tortures were being readied for him. Not that he was worried—he held records for enduring every type of torture imaginable. Suddenly, Stanley noticed that the door had been left unlocked! Carefully, slowly, he turned the doorknob, swinging the door open. No guard outside! With a quick glance he checked out the hallway. Again, no one!

In a moment he was halfway down the hall. Halfway to freedom! That was when he heard voices. Stanley froze. They were coming his way, too close to run! He took a deep breath. *Think,* he told himself. *Think!*

Stanley noticed a door cracked open just opposite from where he stood. He ducked through it, into a darkened room. A faint light came from the window, enough to see. Stanley quickly surveyed his hiding place—it was occupied! A body lay on a bed, unmoving. Probably a prisoner like himself. Post-torture, from the look of it. The voices came nearer, pausing just outside. Stanley slipped against the wall, to where a row of hospital gowns hung from pegs. He let one fall over his head—Stanley, the human coatrack. When it came to avoiding torture, he was a man with no pride.

The door opened; a large woman came in. Stanley held his breath as she walked slowly past, close enough to flutter the gown on his head with the breeze of her passing. She was a rough one, no doubt—probably the commander of the Women's Shock Troops. Or maybe the chief torturer. Through the thin fabric of the gown, Stanley watched her approach the prisoner.

"Don't pretend to be asleep," the woman said, knocking her purse against the bed until the lump under the blanket moved. "The nurse said she just got done examining you."

Stanley frowned. He recognized the woman's voice—and not from any movie either.

"So what did they ask you?" the woman went on. "And what did you tell them?"

"Just what you said to say," a girl answered, her voice thin and flat. Stanley nearly fell over—it was Theresa! And Theresa's mom! When her mom didn't say anything, Theresa added, "I told them I tripped. I fell down the stairs. That's all I told them," she said, her voice breaking, tears filling her throat. "Really!"

"All right, then. But next time you go anywhere without permission," Theresa's mom said in a low voice, "it'll be worse than falling down the stairs. Understand? Next time you just might fall out of an upstairs window. When I tell you to stay home, young lady, you stay home! And I don't want to see those two boys again. Ever!"

Stanley took in a deep breath, holding it, fading back even farther behind the gowns. He didn't have a watch, but it was an absolute sure thing that as he waited for Theresa's mom to leave, he broke every Holding-Your-Breath record ever. He even closed his eyes as she swept past, out the door, mumbling curses that Stanley didn't want to hear, let alone write down and show to Jerry.

Slowly, so slowly that his lungs ached, he let out his breath and took in another. He made no sound at all, nothing that Theresa would notice. Unfortunately, in the absolute silence that filled the room, Stanley could hear Theresa only too well—she was weeping into her pillow, quiet sobs that seemed to go on forever.

As Stanley slowly caught his breath he thought of how she had waved to him that first day and how he hadn't waved back. He thought of how she had saved his life the day he'd come in late for class and how he had never thanked her. He thought of how he should say something to her now, how he should step up to her bed and say something. But what could he say? He wasn't a real hero. Stanley listened to Theresa softly weeping, and he felt tears in his own eyes. *Say something,* Stanley told himself. *Say something!*

Instead, Stanley backed silently toward the door and then into the hallway. He tried his very best to not think at all about what he was doing. In twenty seconds he was again in his own room, in his own bed, the covers pulled up over his head.

the best slave labor camp money can buy

Stanley stayed home the next day and the day after that. But on Thursday, the last day of school, his mom insisted that he go. "Stanley, no one misses the last day of school. You have to go back and face everyone, let all your friends know that you're fully recovered. You have to let them know that even though you made an *unwise decision* . . ." His mom let the words hang there for a few seconds—Stanley imagined how a man with his head on the block felt waiting for the guillotine to drop. "Even though you made an unwise decision," she repeated, "you're willing to stand up like a man and show everyone that you've learned your lesson. You are willing to stand up, apologize, and promise that you'll do a better job next time."

Stanley had no intention of apologizing to anyone. As far as he was concerned, he'd rather run out of class again than stand up like a man and apologize. He didn't even want to stand up like a kid and apologize. The only thing he'd learned was that next time he wouldn't trip in the street. Next time he wouldn't stop running until he reached Canada.

The good part of coming back on the last day of school, Stanley discovered, was that no one even noticed he was there. Everybody was yelling and shouting and running around like they were already on vacation. Everybody, he noticed, except Theresa Wasnicki, who was nowhere to be seen. Stanley felt a little guilty, on account of he wouldn't have known what to say to her anyway, and he was happy that he didn't have to think about it. Only he wondered what had happened to her. What if she'd fallen out a window, like her mother warned her that she might?

"May I remind you," Mrs. Olsen said to the entire class after the first bell had rung, "that while today is the last day of school for this year, it is still a day of school! Furthermore," she continued, rapping her ruler on the top of her desk and frowning, "you do not graduate and will not graduate until you have successfully finished this day. I expect faultless attention and behavior from each and every one of you. Have I made myself perfectly clear?"

"Yes, Mrs. Olsen," the class all said together. And they meant it too, because no one wanted to repeat fifth grade with Mrs. Olsen. Not even Steve Klemp, who had already flunked third and fourth grade, wanted to do that. So all during the day, while every other kid in the entire school was having a class party, making noise, and running around, the kids in Mrs. Olsen's class pretended to be alien pod people. Even when the final bell rang, they all filed out quietly, just as Mrs. Olsen asked them to do, and it was only when they were halfway across the recess playground that someone shouted, "Yeah! No more school! No more Mrs. Olsen!" After that everyone began shouting, *No more school! No more Mrs. Olsen!*

Stanley jumped around and shouted too, only this year he kind of wished that he were going to summer school. Not with Mrs. Olsen, of course. Nobody would be that stupid. But with one of the other teachers. At least then he wouldn't have to go to summer camp. Summer camp had been his mom's big surprise to him for surviving school.

"Don't be silly," his mom said to him when he

arrived home that afternoon and asked once again why he had to go to camp. "It's a wonderful opportunity to meet new friends, learn about the mountains, and try new activities. Why, there isn't a kid in town who wouldn't just love to go to camp with you."

"Why don't they, then?" Stanley asked, on account of yesterday the camp had sent them a list of all the kids on its roster, and Stanley didn't know a single name.

"They can't afford it," his mom explained to him. "It's a very expensive camp. Even Robby's parents can't afford it."

Stanley moaned when he heard this, even though he already knew that Robby wasn't going to camp. He pictured Robby with Jimmy and George riding the bus to the zoo, to the movies, even riding with Mr. Lanorsky to the county fair. Meanwhile, he'd be stuck in a camp where he didn't know a single kid and probably wouldn't say five words for the entire six weeks. By the time he got back, Robby would've probably forgotten who he even was.

"Oh, don't act so gloomy," his mom told him. "You won't be alone. Jerry's going with you. He'll make sure you have fun."

Sure, Stanley thought—like the time he and Jerry were supposed to go bowling, only Jerry took him over to Jennie Moore's house and he had to be the lookout for Jennie's parents the whole time. Or the time Stanley had to park his dad's car in the driveway on account of Jerry had left it in the middle of the street and was too drunk to do anything but lay on the lawn and sing. Or what about the time when Jerry set his bed on fire when he went to sleep with his cigarette still lit and Stanley had to put it out? And now Jerry was going to be the only, the very one and only person in the whole camp whom Stanley could depend on to make sure he had a good time? He moaned again.

"If all you're going to do is mope about, then do it outside, young man. You heard me—outside this very instant. See if any of your friends think going to an exclusive summer camp is such a bad thing!"

Stanley went out the back door, then to his special place under the house to read the Camp Hayseed brochure again. In the ten-page glossy booklet were pictures of smiling kids and friendly looking counselors riding horses, swimming in the camp pool, canoeing on a lake, eating huge plates of spaghetti, and about a hundred other fun activities. What if it was like the Child Labor Camps he'd read about in last Sunday's paper? The paper said that because there were so many people in China and parents couldn't afford to feed their children, that lots of kids were sent off to work camps. Only they weren't called work camps, they were called Children's Play Cooperatives, and just like the Camp Hayseed brochure, the Children's Play Cooperatives had these great-looking pamphlets, with photos of smiling, happy kids having a wonderful time. Only it was all a lie! The children had to work from sunrise to sunset, they almost never got fed, and their families never saw them again. Not that Stanley believed his mom would send him to a slave labor camp. Not on purpose, at least. But what if she didn't know? What if the camp people were lying to her and once his mom and dad had left them there, they would all be chained together and rented out on road gangs? Besides that, if Camp Hayseed was such a great place, why had Stanley heard his mom telling Mrs. Lanorsky that *she* was the one who was looking forward to having a vacation?

All day Friday and Saturday, when every other kid in the known world was out celebrating the beginning of summer, Stanley and Jerry had to stay in and pack. Camp Hayseed had sent them a list of exactly what to bring, how many pairs of pants, how many pairs of socks, even how many pairs of underwear. What type of place would tell you how many pairs of underwear to bring? Stanley imagined a man in a uniform going through his bag, removing his underwear. Counting them. Stanley moaned for the hundredth time that day, then began to carefully count the underwear his mom had laid out for him. He certainly didn't want to start off his stay at Camp Hayseed getting in trouble with the underwear police. That was when he noticed the initials his mom had ironed on: SUKS.

"Mom!" Stanley yelled. "What did you do to my clothes!"

"Don't have a conniption," his mom shouted from her room—she was getting ready for an evening out with their dad. "Celebrating early" is what Jerry called it.

"But, Mom," he said, nearly in tears, "you ironed cusswords into all my underwear!" He quickly checked his shirts, pants, and socks. "Mom, they're on everything! Cusswords, Mom!"

Stanley heard a loud sigh from the other room and then his mom's footsteps hurrying down the hall, into their room. She had her bright red bathrobe wrapped around her. "What?" she said angrily. Her eyebrows arched upward, only it made her face lopsided on account of one eyebrow was long and dark and the other was just an outline and could hardly be seen. "What?" she said again when she noticed Jerry start to giggle. "I'm putting my face on—you have exactly thirty seconds to explain!"

Stanley held up a T-shirt, showing her the ironed-on label. "What on earth is wrong with you, Stanley?" his mom said. "Those are your initials. The camp wants initials on all clothing so that when they do your wash, they can tell whose is whose."

Stanley's mouth bent into a mournful frown. "S-U-K-S?" he said.

"Stanley Uriah Krakow," his mom said impatiently.

"But I never use Uriah. Nobody ever uses Uriah. Besides, what's the extra 'S' at the end for?"

"That's proper English, young man. You don't want people to think you come from an ignorant family, do you? The 'S' shows possession." When Jerry and Stanley both just stared at her, she added, "Stanley Uriah Krakow's. Understand?"

"But it spells 'sucks.' As in, this really sucks."

"Don't you use that language around me, young man! And initials don't spell anything, they're just initials."

"Can't you just put S-K?"

His mom looked at her watch. "Thanks to you, I am now late. And no, I cannot put in new labels, it's out of the question. You don't hear Jerry complaining about it, do you?" With that, she turned and left the room.

Stanley stared morosely at the label on his T-shirt. He could just hear his camp mates asking, *Hey, Sucks, are those your initials, or is that a description of your personality?* They'd probably name him Sucks. *Hey, Sucks, your laundry's here.*

"Don't worry about it," he heard Jerry say.

"Oh, sure. Your initials don't spell 'sucks.'"

"No, but look." Stanley turned toward his brother, who was holding up a pair of blue jeans with JRKS ironed onto them.

"Jerks?" he said. His brother snickered, nodding his head.

"Sucks and Jerks," Jerry said. "And Mom wants everyone to think we come from a good family," he managed to say between snorts of laughter.

"Sucks and Jerks," Stanley repeated. Suddenly, he, too, was laughing. "Like Batman and Robin!"

"Like Tonto and the Lone Ranger!"

"Sucks and Jerks!"

"Jerks and Sucks!" For some reason this was even more hilarious, and they rolled around on the floor, laughing and shouting, "Jerks and Sucks" until their dad came in snapping his belt.

"Quiet down!" he ordered. They covered their mouths, guffaws snorting through their fingers. "I mean it, quiet down! Next time I have to come in here, I'll come in swinging!"

"I thought you sold your golf clubs," Jerry mumbled through his hands.

"What was that?" their dad bellowed.

"Nothing," Jerry said, smiling politely. "Nothing at all."

After their parents left, Jerry got out two black marking pens, and they spent the rest of the evening blacking out letters and packing the clothes so that the labels couldn't be seen by their mom. Every time one of them said, "Jerks and Sucks," they would start laughing again.

Just before the sun set, Stanley took a break from packing. Everyone was outside playing, so he couldn't set any records, but at least he would get to say good-bye to Robby.

"You're going to miss my party," Robby said, looking a little hurt. "Hey," he said when Stanley looked at the ground, blushing, "I'm only kidding you! I'll save you a piece of cake, ha-ha."

He said good-bye to Jimmy and George, also, only they didn't seem to care very much. George shook his hand, but Jimmy just said, "Right! Camp!" The one he really wanted to say good-bye to was Theresa Wasnicki—or at least see if she was all right. If she was all right, he could stop thinking about what a coward he'd been. In fact, if Theresa was all right, maybe he'd been a hero and didn't even know it! Maybe Theresa's mom had actually seen him spying under the gowns and figured she'd better not mess with Theresa now that Stanley was on the case!

Only Teresa wasn't outside her house. Stanley walked past four or five times, but he didn't see her anywhere, and he certainly wasn't going to knock on her door. Not after what her mom had said. He did see that none of the upstairs windows or screens were broken, so at least he figured that she hadn't fallen out.

the road to camp hayseed

The best part about going to camp, if there was a best part, was that their dad drove, on account of their mom hated driving in the mountains. Their dad always played a game when he drove, which he always insisted that he wasn't playing, which totally annoyed their mom. Which, of course, was the best part of the game. At some point during the drive their dad would try to scare them.

"Drive carefully," their mom said about every ten minutes, sitting in the front seat next to their dad. "Don't pass anyone. And don't speed! Remember, it's the first weekend of summer, and every fool in the world is out driving. So for once," she added snidely, "don't be one."

"Not me, my dear," he said, smiling brightly, knowing what was ahead but pretending he didn't.

"Not I," she corrected.

"Neither me nor I nor the both of us together," he said with a wink into the rearview mirror.

As the car climbed slowly up a long, curving incline, Stanley saw a large sign: DEVIL'S LEAP SCENIC OVERLOOK. EXIT WITH CARE. Out the passenger's side window they could see a steep valley cutting right up to the road.

"Irving," his mom warned. But it was too late. The car veered sharply off the road, skidding through the gravel toward the guardrail. "Irving!" she yelled.

"Whoa, boys, look at that drop!" Their dad laughed as they came to a stop at the very edge of the overlook. "Fall off here and you might not hit bottom until the end of summer. Careful, don't lean too far out that window, boys, I think I can feel the car sliding!" That was when he started rocking in his seat, shaking the car.

"Irving!" their mom managed to say through her clamped jaws. "Are you crazy? I swear, I'm going to kill you! Get back onto the road this instant!"

Jerry and Stanley were laughing so hard, they were almost crying. The car was in no actual danger, being still a few feet away from a knee-high steel guardrail, but it was close enough that they could peer straight down into the valley a thousand feet below, which made their giggles come out in wild squeals. "Look at that car down there!" their dad said, sliding over next to their mom to point out a tiny object far, far below. "Camp Hayseeders," he said solemnly. "Too bad. But that means more bunk space for you two."

"Irving!" their mom shouted. "That's a horrible thing to say!"

He laughed again, and the boys howled with him, because when their father was laughing, it was like magic, it was like he was happy and proud and, well . . . in love with them. It was wonderful.

"You are a moron," his mom said. Usually, that would have quieted them all down, but up in the mountains, two feet away from a thousand-foot drop, it only made them laugh even harder. "Three morons!" she said.

Finally, they got back on the road. The turnoff to the camp was only a couple of miles later. Stanley felt his stomach start to roll this way and that as they passed the Camp Hayseed sign. Already, there were groups of kids standing around, staring at the new arrivals. *Or inmates,* Stanley thought. And sure enough, when they pulled up to the cabins, the windows were covered with thick wire mesh. The counselor in charge of Stanley's cabin, Ben, told his mom that the wire was to keep raccoons and other animals out. Stanley tugged on his mom's sleeve as soon as Ben had turned away.

"What?" she said, still mad from the scenic-viewing-area joke. "What is it?"

He did his best to tell her that only a concentration camp would cover the windows with wire mesh. But all she said was, "Stanley, don't you think that if that were true, the prices would be a little cheaper?" Then she turned back to Ben the Counselor and said, "Please excuse Stanley. He has a very active imagination. He thinks you might be running a slave camp here."

They both laughed, of course, his mom and Ben the Counselor. But as soon as his mom and dad had driven off, Stanley noticed that the counselor was no longer even trying to smile. Stanley pretended not to notice—it was always wise to not let evil people know that you were on to them. Once they let their guard down, he could attempt an escape. If they even let him live that long. That was his only job now: to live. No matter what type of tortures they put him through, he must survive. Survive, escape, and warn the world.

mutant horseback riding

On Monday morning, the day after they had arrived at Camp Hayseed, Stanley decided that perhaps the place wasn't a slave labor camp—but he still didn't like being there. During introductions the day before, when the ten kids in his cabin had sat in a circle and told all about themselves, he had turned white and stuttered and hadn't been able to even say where he lived. The only difference from being in school was that Ben didn't crack a ruler over his desk and send him to the principal's office like Mrs. Olsen did. Instead, Ben had started asking him questions that he could answer with just a nod of the head, like, "You're going into sixth grade, right, Stanley?" and "Your birthday's in April, just like Roger's, right?" At least Stanley hadn't started crying. That didn't happen until after bedtime, when he had lain in his bunk wide awake for over two hours, listening to all the other kids snoring.

When Stanley got up Monday morning, he tried to figure out all the pluses and minuses so far. He got out his pocket notebook and his red ballpoint pen and began writing. On the plus side was that none of his cabin mates had seen him crying. Not yet, at least. On the minus side was that they all thought he was a nerd anyway, even before they'd seen him crying. Mostly, the other nine kids just ignored him, which, considering that he could only answer with a nod of his head, wasn't such a bad thing. Even Jerry ignored him. "Isn't that your little brother?" one of Jerry's new camp friends had asked him that morning when they saw Stanley kicking pinecones outside his cabin.

"Not exactly," Jerry told him. "My real brother was abducted by aliens. That," he said, pointing at Stanley, "is what they left in his place. Not very convincing, is it?"

Of course, not knowing Jerry could be a very good thing too. "Isn't that your brother?" Ben the Counselor asked him that evening at supper, after Jerry had been hauled away for shooting spoonfuls of peas at the bear's head mounted on the dinning hall wall. Stanley wanted to say no and tell Ben about how his brother had tragically fallen over the side of Devil's Leap Scenic Overlook and that the boy shooting the peas was just a hitchhiker they had picked up to make his mom feel better. The problem was, by the time he'd practiced the words enough, Ben had turned away and was talking to someone else.

Another minus—and the main thing that made Stanley wonder whether Camp Hayseed's credentials had been checked recently—was the horses. His mom had said that the horses at Camp Hayseed were just like the ones they used in cowboy movies. Wrong! As soon as his parents had left, Stanley had run down to the Camp Hayseed corral, where he was nearly trampled by a herd of giant mutant creatures that almost certainly had escaped from a nuclear dump site. Eight horses moved around the corral, pawing the ground with massive hooves capable of instantly turning a kid's head into SpaghettiOs. Their teeth, which they showed whenever another horse got in their way, were the size of chalkboard erasers and looked sharp enough to snip off a hand with no trouble at all. Stanley was quite sure that there wasn't a cowboy alive who ever took a running jump onto the back of one of these monsters. Not without a springboard.

Monday was "Get to Know Your Camp Day." At the end of it Stanley examined his plus and minus list again. The minus page was nearly full, while the plus page looked like one of Steve Klemp's writing assignments. Tuesday didn't get any better. Tuesday morning, even though Stanley had gotten up five minutes after the final wake-up bell, he found himself first at his cabin's table in the dining hall, where, sure enough, just what he had dreaded lay waiting at his seat: lumpy Cream of Wheat cereal. Stanley was glad no one else was around, for it gave him a chance to take a fork and mash down most of the lumps. Then he noticed that not only wasn't there anyone at his table, there wasn't anyone at any of the tables. The entire dining hall was empty.

Slowly, as kids wandered in, talking about the activities they'd signed up for, Stanley remembered: Ben had read them a list of activities that they could choose from at "sign up time," before breakfast. *Big deal,* he thought, stirring the lumps around in his cereal. So what if he'd forgotten to sign up for anything? What could they do? Kick him out of camp? Hah!

But it was worse than that. Far, far worse.

"All right, Stan!" said Mike, the horseback-riding counselor, upon reading the sign-up list, where Ben had put Stanley's name. "Time to learn some cowboy moves, huh?"

"No," groaned Stanley. He remembered his mom telling Ben how much Stanley wished to learn horseback riding. "No!" he groaned again, but Mike only laughed. Not only that, but because Stanley was the last to arrive, the only horse left was an enormous dirty white beast with a bite out of one ear and a snort powerful enough to send up clouds of dust from the ground. Old Whitey. When Mike led Stanley toward him, the horse sneered and showed his yellow, stained teeth.

"He likes you," Mike announced.

For dinner, Stanley thought. But it was too late to run. Mike hoisted him up by the waist, plopping him atop the mutant creature. Stanley held tight to the saddle while Mike adjusted the stirrups—there were treetops closer to the ground than he was.

As soon as Mike turned toward his own horse, Old Whitey shook his head, sending gobs of slobber flying everywhere. Giant, mutant slobber. "Oh, gross!" some of the nearest kids shouted, then stared at Stanley like it was his fault. Stanley didn't blame them. What would Maverick do if some stranger rode up to him, then doused him with giant horse slobbers?

Mike lined all the horses up, with Stanley in the very back. "Keep the reins in and his head up, okay, cowboy?" Mike said, patting Stanley on the back. "And don't look so worried; Old Whitey's been doing this for a long time. He knows his job." With that, he turned toward the corral entrance, leading the horses out.

One by one, the horses started forward. All but Old Whitey. Stanley said, "Giddyap," though not very loudly, and gave the horse a toss of the reins, but Old Whitey just snorted and stared at the ground.

"Here's the trick," said the corral keeper, coming up behind them. He gave Old Whitey a slap on the rear and yelled, "Hiiiiieee!" The horse bolted forward, which Stanley thought was pretty exciting until he realized that maybe slapping a giant, mutant horse wasn't such a brilliant idea—especially since the only one around to pay for the insult was Stanley.

As soon as they were far enough down the trail that the corral guy couldn't see them, Old Whitey slowed down, then stopped. "Hiiieee!" Stanley said in his best imitation, but Old Whitey paid not the least bit of attention. Instead, with a jerk of his giant, mutant head, he pulled the reins loose and began to leisurely munch on some flowers. Remembering what Mike had told him, Stanley grabbed the reins and yanked—

but that just made Old Whitey angry. He swung his head back, stained yellow chalkboard teeth snapping as they reached for Stanley's leg.

"Help!" Stanley shouted, pulling first one leg then the other out of the stirrups and away from the gigantic teeth. After snapping a few times, Old Whitey went back to the flowers. "Help!" Stanley shouted again, louder this time because the other horses were no longer in sight. "Help!"

At last Mike came galloping back, and just in time too—Old Whitey had finished the last of the flowers and was still looking hungry. "He's trying to eat me!" Stanley said.

Mike grabbed the reins, jerking Old Whitey's head up. "He's not trying to eat you, Stan, he's just trying to scare you."

"Well, it's working!" Stanley said. Then he put his head down, staring at the saddle so that he wouldn't cry.

"Don't worry, cowboy," Mike said. "Sometimes Old Whitey's not in a very good mood. It's not your fault. For now I'm going to keep hold of the reins. You and Old Whitey will ride beside me. Okay?"

Stanley nodded his head but didn't look up, afraid that the other kids would all be laughing. But as he and Mike passed them they all seemed to be having as much trouble with their horses as Stanley was having with Old Whitey. "Keep your feet in the stirrups, Kathy," Mike said to a small girl and, "Don't let go of the reins, Philip." When Stanley glanced to the side, the other kids weren't staring at him, but at their horses, and they didn't look too happy either. Stanley had figured that everyone already knew how to ride a horse, but no one did. Of course, these were giant, mutant horses, he remembered. Even experienced cowboys would have trouble riding these horses.

For the next few miles Old Whitey followed placidly next to Mike's horse, not once trying to pull away or turn and bite Stanley or even to shake his head and toss giant mutant wads of spit. "Good boy," Stanley said softly after a couple of minutes. "Good Old Whitey." He bent carefully forward, patting Old Whitey's neck. Old Whitey's hair was prickly, like the brush Stanley's mom used on him every Sunday to hold down his cowlick, and he smelled a lot like Jerry's gym shorts. Still, Stanley continued petting the horse and whispering nice things into his ear. Maybe he and Old Whitey could get to be friends.

Stanley imagined Old Whitey standing at the corral fence, waiting for him, nuzzling Stanley's neck when he finally appeared. Maybe by the end of camp Stanley would be the only kid Old Whitey would let ride him. Maybe he would even do tricks, but just for Stanley. Everyone in the entire camp would say what an absolutely amazing horse trainer Stanley was, and when ESPN came to film Old Whitey's total transformation, everyone there would cheer. Mike and Ben would give interviews saying what a pleasure it had been to have Stanley in their camp and how much they had learned from him, and Robby and Theresa, and even George and Jimmy, would watch it all on TV.

Stanley didn't notice the horses filing one by one back into the corral or Mike getting off his horse and letting go of Old Whitey's reins. "Good boy," Stanley went on chanting, petting the horse's grizzled mane and thinking about how by the end of camp, instead of using the corral gate, old Whitey and he would probably just jump the fence. "Good boy," he said again. Then Stanley yelled, "Hey!" as he saw Old Whitey's head bend around, trying to bite his leg. "Hey!"

Just before the huge, mutant teeth could eat Stanley's boot, Mike grabbed Stanley and swung him to the ground. "That is not very nice!" he said to the horse, only he had to jump back before he'd even finished, on account of Old Whitey took a snap at him, too.

For the first time that day Stanley smiled. "I think he's just trying to scare you," he told Mike.

176

"Very funny," Mike said. "Very funny. By the way, Stan, guess what Ben signed you up for this afternoon?" He smiled broadly. "You want me to save Old Whitey for you?"

One thing was for sure, Stanley thought: He would never be late for activities sign-up again. And from then on, he was taking pottery and crafts.

23

soaring

The only thing wrong with waking up early for activities sign-up, Stanley soon found out, was that sometimes he didn't. Sometimes he was so completely exhausted from staying up half the night protecting himself and the rest of the cabin from Prehistoric Flying Beetle Blood Suckers that he slept right through the final morning wake-up bell. Ben's rule was that he would shake a kid once to help him get up, but after that, as he said, he approved of everyone's inalienable right to fail, whatever that meant. Sometimes Stanley would even sleep right through breakfast—not that he was missing much; all they usually got was lumpy hot cereal.

The problem with lumpy hot cereal was that it made Stanley throw up. He told this to Ben the very first morning and asked why he couldn't just have cold cereal, but Ben told him that the camp had assured all the parents that a hot meal would be served three times a day, and, after all, cold cereal was cold.

"What if we heat it up?" one of the kids had asked Wednesday morning.

"Or put the hot cereal in a blender?" another kid put in. "My mom always puts it in a blender before I eat it. Why can't we do that?" Looking around the table, Stanley had been surprised to find that most of his companions were carefully searching through the mush, removing the many lumps. That was when Ben had told everyone at Muskrat Table, where all his kids sat, that the lumps in the cereal were healthy and that crunching them up was good exercise for the teeth. And besides that, he was tired of hearing them whine. He was especially tired of hearing certain kids whine.

"I won't mention names," he said, staring with a frown at Stanley, who, unfortunately, was sitting almost directly across from the counselor, "but from now on, if you don't want hot cereal for lunch, too, you'd better eat it for breakfast. All of it!" he added, his eyes still on Stanley. "Now!"

Stanley did his best to smile. "That's the attitude, Stanley!" he heard Ben say. "Everyone, look at Stanley. He's no wimp. Go ahead, Stanley, dig in!"

So Stanley dug in. The first bite was smooth and creamy, and Stanley swallowed it without effort. Ben the Counselor was beaming at him. *Who knows?* Stanley thought, digging in for a second bite, *I might get to like camp cereal.* He might get to be the camp cereal record holder, he might even . . . Stanley felt a lump touch his tongue, then jump toward his throat, trying to choke him. Before he could stop it, the entire mouthful of cereal sprayed across the table, quickly followed by the rest of Stanley's breakfast.

"Eww! Gross!" said Tommy, who sat next to Ben. The next thing he said was, "Oh boy, I don't feel—" But he never finished, on account of he threw up too. Then everyone started throwing up. After a while even Ben threw up. Pretty soon kids at other tables started throwing up, and anybody who hadn't was running outside, where most of them threw up in the bushes. Also, there was a tangle getting out the door, and five girls had to be taken to the nurse for bruises and cuts.

The only good part of it was that Stanley got to write home telling his mom all about it, leaving nothing out. Let her read that to her friends! Stanley also told her about the giant mutant horses. Of course, when he wrote to Robby, the story got changed a little. It was still true, of course—all about how the giant mutant horse called Old Whitey, who had never been successfully ridden, finally met his match. He even wrote to Theresa, although he couldn't think of much to say, except that he was sorry she wasn't there for the last day of school and that he hoped she was having a fun summer. He wanted to sign it *Your friend*, only he didn't; he just wrote his name. After thinking about it for a while he added, *I was in Mrs. Olsen's class with you. I sat two rows over.*

One thing he didn't write anyone about was the Prehistoric Flying Beetle Blood Suckers. He didn't want to scare anyone, especially himself. Also, he thought the Prehistoric Flying Beetle Blood Suckers might be smarter than they looked—if they caught on that he knew about them, he might be the first to go. So far no one from his cabin had succumbed to them, but that was only because Stanley stayed up late every night on guard duty.

On the first night of camp Ben had told the kids in the cabin that the wire screens over the windows were put there to prevent any animals from getting in, so everyone should feel perfectly safe. He even went outside and tested each window, rattling them and banging on them, to show everyone just how safe they all were. Safe from everything that hadn't already gotten inside, Stanley figured. And sure enough, as soon as Ben turned off the lights, the prehistoric monster beetles started flying around, buzzing loudly as they zoomed by. Ben told everyone that they were harmless, so go to sleep. He even stayed in the middle of the cabin until the buzzing stopped—as if that were a good thing, which Stanley knew it wasn't. All it meant was that the beetles had all picked out their bedmates for the night and were now waiting for eyes to close. "See?" Ben told them. "Perfectly harmless." Of course, Ben had his own room, and Stanley noticed that the door to it was kept tightly shut.

Stanley watched the beetles carefully, his covers pulled up to his chin, only his eyes moving. Like all evil night dwellers, Stanley knew that they were essentially cowards and wouldn't make a move until everyone was asleep. His staying awake was all that saved them from absolute destruction!

At first he thought the beetles might be flesh-eaters, but wary observation showed that the beetles didn't have teeth. Instead, they relied upon two large suckers that came out of their mouths. Stanley reasoned that they worked like straws and that once the beetles had inserted them into an arm or leg—or to be really quick, probably a neck—all that Ben would find the next morning would be a pair of pajamas covering skin and bones. For all Stanley knew, they might even suck up those! They might be hideously smart and even fold up the pajamas. Now that he thought of it, Stanley remembered seeing neatly folded pajamas in some of the other cabins. Ben had even pointed them out on the way back from breakfast, saying how tidy they looked. Was Ben in on it, or was he just a fool? Did anyone even suspect what was going on?

So that was how Stanley ended up running toward the activity sign-up area one morning about a week into camp with one sneaker held in his hand, the other flapping untied, and his T-shirt on backward, all because of staying up late to protect his cabin. By the time he got there, only two activities were left: Mutant Horseback Riding and the Trampoline. Both were perilously dangerous, but at least the trampoline instructor, Wendy, didn't laugh when she saw Stanley's name, which was what Mike always did. Laugh and saddle up Old Whitey. So Stanley signed up for the trampoline.

The trampoline that the camp used was huge, the kind that sent a kid a minimum of ten feet into the air no matter how gently he jumped. The first lesson that

Wendy taught the class was how to stop, only it looked to Stanley that if a kid did what Wendy was telling them all to do, his legs would instantly break. He nodded, thinking, *Yeah, that sure would stop a kid from jumping, all right.* Stanley quickly decided that a much better way of stopping was to never start, which was why he volunteered to be one of the safety people surrounding the trampoline, ready to catch anyone who bounced the wrong way. There had to be a minimum of five safeties before anyone could start jumping. All Stanley knew was that he sure wouldn't go into a pool that needed five lifeguards.

After learning to stop, the first lesson for each jumper was how to do a sit bounce, which was when a person jumped up, put his legs out and landed on his bottom, and then bounced up onto his feet again. Before going to the next lesson, a kid had to do a minimum of thirty sit bounces in a row. Almost nobody got to thirty. And the way Stanley had it planned, he would never have to try.

"Your turn," Wendy said to Stanley.

"Oh . . . I have to go to the rest room first. Okay?"

"No problem," Wendy said, only when he started walking back to his cabin, she added, "Stanley, we have a bathroom right here. It's behind the equipment shed."

"Oh," Stanley said. "Thanks." He walked to the bathroom, locking himself inside for what he hoped would be the rest of the activity period, only one of the other kids from the trampoline class knocked on the door.

"Hurry up!" the kid said, and Stanley could tell that he meant it. Stanley sighed. He didn't know if it was an official rule or not, but you just couldn't lock someone out of the bathroom if he really needed to get in. So he walked back to the trampoline, where he found the whole class waiting for him.

"Up you go," Wendy said, helping him onto the massive, jiggly black surface.

Just moving to the center of the trampoline proved to be highly hazardous, for no matter how slowly Stanley moved, the rubbery surface reacted with violent waves, threatening to bounce Stanley into one of the safeties. Around him he heard soft, tittering laughter. *Great,* Stanley thought—whole new areas of humiliation were opening up in his life.

Stanley reached the center of the trampoline still standing, which should have been enough of an accomplishment. But, apparently, more was expected. The tittering died down; however, Stanley recognized the quiet as just a period of waiting and watching for something even funnier to happen. *The Stanley*

Krakow Comedy Hour was about to begin. "Come on, champ," Wendy said. "Time to jump!"

Stanley was about to say that he just couldn't when Wendy pushed down on her section, forcing a huge ripple across the trampoline surface. Without thinking about it, Stanley's knees bent, and the trampoline bounced him into the air. He came down on his feet, his knees bending again, and this time shot upward, soaring.

Something utterly and absolutely amazing happened then: Stanley realized he wasn't afraid. He didn't know how or why, only that he felt something different in him, something, well, different. The wind lifted his hair as he rose, tickling his ears, and then there was an indescribable pause at the top, when he was neither up nor down and when the world seemed to halt around him, holding its breath. Then his legs went out, he landed on his bottom, he bounced up again, and he landed on his feet, again and again and again. At first he heard everyone counting— "One, two, three . . ."— but then it was as if they all disappeared. It was as if everything disappeared, everything but the wind in his face, the pine trees rising and falling around him, the sun at the top of each jump, the shadows at the bottom. And what he thought about was the time at the hospital when Uncle Alan had tossed him into the air, about how he had known, absolutely known that Uncle Alan would catch him, that he would never let him fall. The trampoline felt the same way. Like he was finally safe. Like he had been waiting for this all his life.

"Stanley," he heard Wendy calling, and then he forgot where he was and tumbled sideways. "Stanley." Wendy laughed as she helped him down. "Did you forget where you were?" Stanley blushed. "I'm sorry I had to stop you," she said, still laughing, "but it's time for lunch. Besides, I think I was the only one still counting."

"Did I get to thirty?" Stanley asked.

"Thirty? Stanley, you got to three hundred. Three hundred twenty-eight, to be exact. That's a new camp record."

"A record?" Stanley repeated. "A real record?"

Wendy laughed again and messed up Stanley's hair with her hand. "Yes, a real record. What other kind is there? Would you like to come back this afternoon?" she asked. "I have the older kids then, but you should do all right."

"Okay," Stanley said dully. "A record," he mumbled, walking away. "A real record."

Stanley ate lunch quickly and hurried back to the trampoline area, on account of he began to think that he hadn't heard Wendy right and that it would be just too embarrassing if she forgot who he was in front of the older kids. He walked around and around the trampoline, and the more he walked, the more he felt sure that he'd made a mistake, that Wendy couldn't possibly have wanted him to come to the afternoon class. He was about to leave when she showed up.

"My champion," she said. Then she laughed and messed his hair up again. "I'm glad you got here early, Stanley. You know, I think you're going to be a real whiz on the tramp." Stanley smiled and stared at the ground, feeling the heat come to his face. "Well, I know you're good at sit bounces," she said when a few other kids had arrived. "Want to try stomach bounces?" Stanley just shrugged. One of the reasons he liked Wendy was because she knew that a shrug meant *yes*. "Okay, then, up you go," she said.

Even though Wendy had explained that stomach bounces were much harder than sit bounces, as soon as Stanley started, it was just like before—it was like he was flying, it was like Uncle Alan was right there with him and he could do anything he wanted. He never had to think about jumping or landing, it just happened. After a while Stanley started to notice what the camp looked like from the air. He could see almost every cabin; he could see kids going in and coming back out. Then he noticed how his hair floated above his head at the top of every jump and how it felt like he was being rocked to sleep every time the tramp pushed him back up into the air. Not that he remembered what it felt like to be rocked to sleep, but if he could remember, he was sure that it would feel just like the trampoline.

"Hey!" one of the kids shouted. "Doesn't anyone else get a turn?" Suddenly, Stanley was aware of about twenty kids standing around, all watching him, and he tumbled to a stop.

"We never interrupt anyone who is in the process of setting a camp record," Wendy admonished the kid who had spoken. Then, to Stanley, "You did great," she said, giving him a big smile. Stanley just stared at her, feeling the breath stopping in his lungs, waiting. "Four hundred and ten," she told him.

"A record?" he asked.

"A record," she assured him happily.

Every day after that, and despite every effort on the part of the Prehistoric Flying Beetle Blood Suckers to make him late, Stanley showed up at sign-up bright and early to register for trampoline jumping. He set bigger and bigger records, for sit bounces and stomach bounces, for knee drops and combinations, even for flips—regular flips, flips onto his stomach, flips onto his knees, and back flips.

"Do you think ESPN will come out to film me?" he asked Wendy one day. But she just laughed.

"I don't think so, champ. But I'll take some photos and send them to you once I get them developed."

"Next year," Stanley said, his face serious, "I bet ESPN will film me. I'm going to send them one of your photos. That way, not only can I set a camp record, I can set a world record."

"Who knows?" Wendy said, smiling. "Who knows?"

Stanley wrote to his mom and dad about his amazing record-setting abilities and about how Wendy the Counselor said that next year ESPN would come out to film him. He wrote Robby all about it too. And he sent Theresa a photo that one of the kids had taken of him on the trampoline. *I'm a little blurred,* he wrote on the back of it, *but it's me, Stanley. In case you don't remember.*

grand master stanley krakow

The high point of camp, or at least what the counselors thought of as the high point, came at the beginning of the last week, when, for three days, everyone was divided into teams: Red, Blue, and Green. The teams competed all day long, in all activities, and the winner after three days would get extra ice cream at dinner for the remainder of camp. To Stanley, getting divided into teams was almost as good an idea as reading-aloud period. First of all, he was always the absolutely, positively last kid to get picked. And second, he usually stunk so bad at everything that even his own team rooted against him. To make matters even worse, Ben decided to pass out the envelopes containing either a red, blue, or green circle just before dessert was served—creamy chocolate pudding that never, ever had a lump in it and that was just about the best part of camp. But watching everyone rip open their envelopes and shout out the color of their team made Stanley's stomach upset. He stuck the unopened envelope deep into his pocket, then pushed his pudding to the side.

"So what team are you on?" the kid next to him asked. Jason, Stanley remembered—Jason never talked to Stanley, or at least not since the day Stanley had thrown up all over him.

"I don't know." Stanley shrugged. "I haven't looked yet."

"Well, look already!"

Stanley dug the envelope out of his pocket and tore it open, removing the card. "Blue," he announced.

"Yes!" Jason shouted. He pushed back his chair and danced in a circle, stabbing the air with a fist.

Stanley just stared at him. Finally, he said, "So you're on Red? Or Green?"

Jason stopped dancing, his forehead scrunching up. "No. I'm on Blue, like you." When Stanley still didn't say anything, Jason went on: "We're teammates. Get it? This is a good thing."

"Why?" was all Stanley could think of to say.

Again, Jason's forehead wrinkled. "Well, because . . . because . . . gee whiz, Stanley, everyone knows that nobody can beat you on the trampoline. That means Blue starts out one hundred points ahead." Jason's eyes suddenly narrowed. "You're sure you're a Blue?" he asked.

Stanley wanted to ask if Jason was making fun of him, only he didn't, on account of that was just what people who were making fun of you wanted you to ask. Instead, he silently held up his blue card for inspection.

Jason's smile immediately returned. "Great!" he said, slinging an arm over Stanley's shoulder. "We're gonna win, buddy! Not a doubt in my mind."

After dinner Stanley walked back to the cabin with his new friend, unable to say a word. He kept glancing down at the paper in his hand, then at the one Jason held, just to make sure he had heard Jason right. On the way there another kid, Elias, ran up to them. "Blue?" he asked hopefully.

Jason nodded. "Both of us," he added when Elias continued to stare at Stanley.

"All right!" he said, putting his palm out for slaps. Then he, too, slung an arm around Stanley. "All for one and one for all!" Elias cheered, but Stanley was too amazed to speak.

All that night Stanley worried about what was happening. It seemed too good to be true. And, of course, it was. The very next morning, before the beginning of trampoline class, Wendy said, "Stanley, I need to speak with you." Immediately, Stanley began to worry, because the only time adults said "I need to speak with you" was when something wasn't right. Wendy took him over next to the equipment shed, where no one else could hear. "Stanley, the counselors all met last night, and some of them don't think it's right to let you compete on the tramp. They say that you can compete in all the other activities but not on the tramp."

"But . . . but . . ." Stanley turned away, feeling the tears hot against his cheeks. "But I'm not good at anything else!" he blurted out. "I'm good at this! It isn't fair!" he shouted. Then he turned and ran.

Wendy caught up with him at his cabin, but only after he had climbed into his bunk and pulled the covers up over his head. "Stanley," she said.

"You can't come in here, it's a boys' cabin!" he yelled.

"There's no one else in here."

"I don't want to talk to you, anyway! I don't have to talk to cheaters, and that's all you are, a bunch of stupid cheaters! Finally, finally, I'm good at something, and you say I can't do it! It's not fair!"

"That's exactly what I told the other counselors," Wendy agreed. "I told them that it just wasn't the right thing to do, penalizing a camper for doing his very best with the talents God had given him. And I told them that I would quit right then and there unless something could be done."

Stanley peeked out from under his covers. "You did?"

"I certainly did. And I meant it! So we reached a compromise. Want to hear it?" Stanley shrugged, and Wendy said, "Good. Because I think you'll like it."

She opened the sports bag that she always carried and brought out a sheet of paper. It was decorated with an ornamental frame along the edges and a picture of kids running, along with CAMP HAYSEED SPECIAL AWARD in big letters at the top. "'This is to certify,'" Wendy read, "'that Stanley Krakow has set the following camp records.'" Then she read off every one of his trampoline records, including a few that he didn't even know he had set. "'We are pleased to have such a talented trampolinist in our camp, and though Mr. Krakow, because of his obvious superiority, will not be competing in the Camp Hayseed Annual Summer Games trampoline events, we would like to announce that Stanley will give a demonstration of his skills directly after the trampoline competition is completed.'"

Wendy stopped reading and handed the certificate to Stanley. "So what do you think?" she asked after he had time to read it for himself.

"A demonstration?" he asked.

"That's right," she said in an encouraging voice. "Just you. It might be the perfect place, you know, to set a world record. I've already called the people who compile the *Guinness Book of World Records* to find out what the records are. So . . . is it a deal?"

"Okay," he finally said, "a deal."

The trampoline competition was on the last day of the Summer Games. In fact, it was the last event of the last day. So far Stanley had performed miserably in all his scheduled events. In archery he'd come in dead last, failing to even hit the target. He did a bit better in pottery, where, though it hadn't won anything, his wobbly bowl inscribed with his mother's initials at least had not cracked apart during firing. But then, in the three-legged sack race, Stanley had fallen over backward before he'd even taken a step, and he and his teammate had become the only kids in history to finish the race without ever getting past the starting line. He thought maybe he shouldn't even go to the trampoline competition, only Wendy found him and made him sit in a chair she had specially marked with a sign reading

RESERVED FOR STANLEY KRAKOW, TRAMPOLINE MAS-
TER.

There were six events scheduled for the trampoline, and it took most of the afternoon before the first-,
second-, and third-place awards were given out.
Finally, though, it was over. Stanley was secretly wish-
ing that they could all just go back to their cabins, that
Wendy and everyone else would just forget about him.
Instead, Wendy smiled at Stanley, messed up his hair,
and announced in a loud voice, "Now, campers, as you
all know, we have a special treat. Stanley Krakow, the
grand master of Camp Hayseed trampolinists, will be
attempting to break the *Guinness Book* world record for
most knee-to-stomach-to-standing jumps for persons
twelve and under, which is . . . one thousand and four."

With that, Stanley was helped onto the trampoline. He wished Wendy had picked something easier,
like sit bounces, only she had said that the record for
those was about five thousand and that it would take
too long to do them. The problem was, his record in
knee-stomach-stand bounces was only two hundred
twenty-eight.

"One!" everyone shouted as he began. "Two!
Three!" Only this time, instead of getting tired like
they usually did, they just got louder and louder.

"One hundred!" they yelled.

"Two hundred!"

When he passed his old record of two hundred twenty eight, everyone cheered. Stanley grinned. At least he had set a new camp record.

"Three hundred!" they shouted. It seemed to Stanley that they were getting even louder, if that was possible. Then he noticed that the crowd was growing. At the top of every jump he could see more and more kids walking over to join them. The higher he went, the more people he saw streaming toward the trampoline area. Some of them were even running!

"Four hundred!"

"Five hundred!"

"You can do it, Stanley!" someone yelled. Stanley recognized the voice—it was Jerry's! On his next jump he looked around the crowd, saw Jerry in the front, waving. "Come on, Stanley!" he coached.

And then half of the kids started shouting, "Stanley! Stanley!" over and over again, while the rest counted.

"Six hundred!

"Stan-ley! Stan-ley!"

"Seven hundred!"

"Stan-ley! Stan-ley!"

"Eight hundred!" That was when he almost fell. The entire crowd immediately grew silent. Stanley recovered, though just barely. Up until then he hadn't been tired, or at least he hadn't thought about it. But suddenly, he was aware of how rubbery his legs felt. Also, his foot, which he had twisted when he'd stumbled, began to throb.

Wendy shouted to him, "It's okay to stop, champ," but he could barely hear her, as the kids had all started chanting again. He looked around at the huge circle of faces watching him, roaring out the count, calling his name. Stop? That would be quitting. Would Dark Man ever quit? Would the Famous Stanley Krakow ever quit? Never!

"Nine hundred!"

"Stan-ley! Stan-ley!"

"One thousand!" Even the counselors joined in.

At one thousand five Stanley fell flat onto the tramp and couldn't get up, but everyone kept cheering and cheering anyway. Finally, Wendy helped roll him off.

"Stan-ley! Stan-ley!" everyone kept cheering. As Stanley walked through the crowd he saw Jerry cheering along with everyone else. "Way to go, bro!" he shouted.

"Is that really your brother?" one of the kids asked him.

"The very truth," Jerry answered, a wide smile covering his face. "Fact is, I taught him everything he knows!"

stanley the mole

"Zamborific!" Robby said, reading Stanley's certificate. "Totally, absolutely, and fantastically
Zamborific! Man, Stan, I wish I knew where a trampoline was around here. Hey!" he yelled at Jimmy, who
was bouncing a ball off a garage door on the other side
of the street. "Jimmy! Come here and look at Stan's
award."

Jimmy grabbed the ball, then trotted over to join
them. After Robby had explained where Stanley had
been and what the award was about, Jimmy just stood
there, staring at the certificate, his head bobbing up

and down like it was attached to a spring. "Cool," he finally said, looking up, his eyes blank. "Only, uh . . . what's a trampoline?"

"A trampoline, you know," Robby explained. "You jump on it. It's, like, made of stretched rubber, you go flying into the air."

"Oh, yeah!" Jimmy said, nodding again. "Cool!" he said, holding his palm out to Stanley for a slap. "Really." Then his face got confused again, his eyebrows tilting down. "Only where are you going to find one of those things around here?"

Robby just shrugged. Stanley stared at his shoes. "Guess Stan'll just have to wait for the national championships," Robby said.

Jimmy tossed his ball into the air, then caught it. "National championships," he repeated doubtfully. Then he added, "I mean, cool award and everything, only isn't it sort of dumb, being a champion of something nobody even knows about? It's not on TV, is it?" When neither Robby nor Stanley said anything, Jimmy did his best to smile, only not much came of it. "Well, see you," he said as he turned away, heaving the ball high into the air and running after it.

Robby wrapped his arm around Stanley's shoulder. "Hey, a champion is a champion," he said. "Come on, let's get an ice cream. Mom's got a box hidden in her

Robert-proof freezer. . . . Robert-proof." Robby grinned. "But is it Stanley-proof, I ask you? Is it?" When Stanley smiled, Robby jumped in the air. "Yes!" he shouted. "We feast!"

Jimmy, as it turned out, had a point. Within a week, even Robby had stopped talking about Stanley's trampoline accomplishments. Not only that, but Stanley received a letter from the publisher of the *Guinness Book of World Records* stating that his trampoline feat had not been properly documented and that further documentation was needed before he could be officially listed in their records. The only good thing about the letter was that he'd been the one to take the mail in that day, so at least no one else saw it. Stanley took it into the backyard and burned it. After that he took a walk. He didn't notice any ESPN vans around—they'd probably given up on him too.

He walked down his old rock-kicking course, which was what he'd done every day since he'd returned from camp. Only he didn't kick any rocks. And like every day before, Theresa Wasnicki was nowhere to be seen. He wanted to go up and knock on the door, find out how she was and ask if she'd gotten his letters. Except there was now a lock on the front gate. Besides, what would he do if Mrs. Wasnicki answered the door? Of course, Mrs. Wasnicki might have forgotten about him by then. Stanley thought of his special award certificate—after all, everyone else had forgotten about him.

Stanley stared morosely at the ground, kicking the sidewalk. Then, under a bush next to the Wasnickis' mailbox, Stanley noticed a part of his face. And then another part. Stanley bent down. It was the photo he'd sent Theresa, the one of him on the trampoline—some of it, at least. Only a few pieces were left; the others must have blown away.

"Hey!" a voice yelled. "What are you doing to our mail?" Stanley popped up, whacking his head on the mailbox as he rose. Tears filled his eyes. He turned in a circle, rubbing his head and looking for whoever had yelled at him. The street was empty. The sidewalk was empty. The Wasnickis' yard was empty.

"Hey!" the voice yelled again. Then shoes smacked the sidewalk in front of him, the tree limb above him waving up and down. Stanley found Theresa Wasnicki staring into his eyes, arms crossed, foot tapping. Waiting. Dumbly, he held out the pieces of the photo.

Theresa took them, working the pieces until they fit together. Puzzled, she turned the partial photo over, seeing what he'd written: *it's me, Stanley. In case you don't remember.* Theresa looked up, even more puzzled. "I don't get it," she finally said. "You're tearing up pictures of yourself and tossing them around our mailbox? Well, I guess that would be hard to forget, all right."

Stanley turned a deep shade of red. "I mailed it to you," he mumbled. And then, when Theresa didn't say anything, he added, "From camp."

"Oh!" Theresa laughed. "I get it! You see, my mom thinks that she's the only one who lives here."

"So . . ." Stanley slowly worked it out for himself. "It was your mom who tore it up?"

"Yep. Tears up all my mail." Theresa smiled and shrugged at the same time. "Some people are just like that. Go figure," she said. "So what're you doing? In the photo?" she asked, turning the pieces first one way, then another. "It looks like maybe someone threw you off a cliff."

"I was on a trampoline."

"A trampoline?" Theresa practically sang. "I love trampolines! We have one, you know," she added proudly. "Come on, I'll show you!"

She scrambled up one of the trees that lined the street, then along a low, thick branch that passed over the hedge and fence surrounding the Wasnickis' yard. "Well, come on," she said when Stanley didn't move. "It's easy!" When Stanley still didn't move, she added, "I don't have a key for the lock on the gate—that's why I do it this way. Okay?"

Stanley followed carefully. The drop into her yard was only a few feet, but even then, Stanley wouldn't have done it if Theresa hadn't been watching. But she was, so he did.

"Maybe I can help you look for your key," Stanley suggested hopefully.

Theresa just shrugged. "My mom doesn't want me going out when she's not here," she told him. "She doesn't even want me out of the house, but I solved that, too! I'm probably a genius!" She laughed. "See the canvas ladder hanging from the porch roof?" Stanley hadn't really seen it, but with Theresa pointing, he noticed what looked like a net hanging down, fluttering in the breeze. "My mom doesn't even know it's there; the people who lived here before us put it on the roof in case a fire blocked the stairs. I just hop out of my window, unroll the ladder, and I'm free! Now come on, let me show you the trampoline before she gets back!"

Stanley wanted to point out that if her mom didn't want her own daughter playing outside on the trampoline, what would she do if she caught him on it? Only there was nothing to worry about, on account of the trampoline was covered with a tarp and leaning up against the house. Theresa lifted the tarp, showing Stanley the trampoline, which was ready to use except for it being on its side against the house.

"So what do you think? Yeah, I know," she said before Stanley had a chance to talk, "it'd be a whole lot better if we'd lay it down. Only my mom says I might get injured. Might have fun is more like it."

Stanley looked at it, pushing the trampoline cover. "Nice," he said. And it was too. Though he couldn't be sure, it looked like the same type they used at Camp Hayseed. "When do you get to use it?" Stanley imagined himself setting stupendous records, camera trucks lining the street. He imagined Jimmy giving him the thumbs-up sign and shouting, *Cool!* He imagined the *Guinness Book of World Records* sending a special representative out to apologize to him.

"Only when my aunt Helen, my mom's sister, comes to visit," Theresa told him. "She's the one who bought it for me, so a day before she gets here, we set it up. It's like a big production; my parents really try to impress her. That's because she started a business and got rich, and all my mom ever got was my dad. Aunt Helen's also really nice, but they don't care because—" Theresa stopped in midsentence, her head tilting, listening. "Oh, drat!" she said. "That's my mom's car pulling into the driveway!" Stanley listened but heard nothing. "I have to get inside!" she said, already running for the porch. Over her shoulder she said, "Whatever you do, don't let her see you!" Then she was up the ladder and onto the porch roof. With a single pull, the ladder was out of sight.

Stanley heard a car door slam. He looked around for somewhere to hide, but he saw nothing. Even if there was a place, his legs felt frozen, unable to move. All he could think about was Theresa's mom at the hospital, the meanness of her voice—and that might have been her bright side, for all Stanley knew. He jerked up the tarp of the trampoline, then thought better of it. If he hid under there, he might not get away until Aunt Helen arrived. Unable to think, Stanley dashed for a bush next to the chain-link fence on the side of the house. He was out of sight, but there was nowhere to go—in both directions grass grew right up to the fence, cutting off any escape.

The Wasnickis' front door slammed loudly, and then Theresa's mom could be heard shouting, "Where are you? Come and help put the groceries away! And I mean now!"

Stanley imagined how it would end. In two or three years they would find his bones next to the fence. Or maybe they'd find that he'd fallen out of an upstairs window. His stomach growled, reminding him that it was nearly dinnertime. "Shhh!" he whispered. His stomach only growled louder. He thought of making a dash for the branch he'd climbed in on, but Mrs. Wasnicki might be waiting on the porch. Even if she just saw him from a window, she'd know, and then what would happen to Theresa?

Stanley punched angrily at the ground. His fist sank into the spongy soil. He punched again, smiling, and began to dig. At first the dirt moved away from the fence in large clumps, but as the hole deepened, the ground grew harder. Still, what choice did he have? His fingers began to ache; his fingernails felt as if they were being pulled off. Stanley tried using sticks to dig with, but there weren't any big enough to really help, and he certainly wasn't going to go looking for larger ones. So he kept working at it, and after what seemed like hours, he was able to wiggle under the fence and into the hedge on the other side. Stanley crept on his stomach back to the sidewalk, then got up and ran all the way home.

"Don't come a step farther!" his mom yelled as he opened the door. For a moment Stanley thought that Mrs. Wasnicki must have called her. But then she said, "You go right back out, mister, and undress in the garage! I've never seen anything so filthy in my whole life! People must think I gave birth to a mole!"

Stanley gave a sigh of relief as he stepped back outside. He hadn't realized how dirty he was until then. His white T-shirt was nearly black, leaves and clots of dirt hung from his hair and filled his ears, and his fingers looked like some type of alien slime mold. He only wished he had a mirror. *Or a camera,* he thought—that would work even better. He certainly couldn't just waste such great good looks. Stanley turned, running toward Robby's house. He'd have a camera!

"You snuck out under the fence?" Robby said. "No way!" Stanley nodded proudly. "The adventures of Stanley Krakow," Robby said. "Now turn a little away from me. I want to get a good shot of your ear. You know it's filled with dirt?" Robby leaned closer, squinting. "I think there's a worm in there! Man, Stan, next time come and get me first!"

getting ready for school

The next week, ten days before school began, Stanley went with his mom to the store, where he bought a brand-new, deluxe, college-edition notebook, the kind that came with three hundred sheets of lined paper and ten subject dividers, two each in red, blue, green, yellow, and orange. He also bought five pens and five pencils, a ruler, a compass, two erasers, a pencil sharpener, eight book covers with a place for his name and address on each one, and two hundred extra sheets of paper, just in case.

"You must be the biggest nerd in your whole class,"

Jerry said when he saw all the school supplies lying on Stanley's bed. "I am soooo glad I go to a different school."

Stanley ignored him, on account of there were some things in life that were worse than Jerry. Like walking into a new classroom late on the first day of school and trying to pretend that everyone wasn't staring. That was definitely worse, which was why he had also bought an alarm clock, so that he would be sure to get to school at least half an hour early. This year, Stanley had thought of everything. This year there was absolutely nothing that could go wrong!

So that Jerry wouldn't laugh at him any more than he already had, Stanley waited until he left before taking the three hundred sheets of paper out of his notebook and putting them on his desk, along with his two hundred extra sheets. Then he divided them into subjects, and so he would never get them mixed up, even if someone knocked the notebook out of his hands and the pages came loose in a big jumble, he numbered each and every page according to subject, such as *Math 1, Math 2, Math 3,* and so on. He then printed in large letters on the subject dividers all of his subjects, even music and art. Next, he borrowed his mom's kitchen timer and practiced the Pledge of Allegiance for an entire hour, until the words were so perfectly clear that no one would ever make fun of the way he said it again.

For sure, nothing could be worse than forgetting the Pledge of Allegiance on the first day of school. Except throwing up on Steve Klemp, of course. That was worse. He knew all about how bad throwing up on Steve Klemp could be, because that was exactly what had happened on the first day of school last year. Not only did Stanley get in massive amounts of trouble for throwing up on Steve Klemp, but he had to go to the nurse's office, which was, if possible, even worse than the principal's office. At the principal's office he usually just got bawled out and told to sit in the detention room, but the nurse always and without fail called up his mom. Only that day his mom hadn't been home, so the nurse called up his dad instead, and his dad had to leave work to take him home.

"You did what?" his dad said when the nurse told him that Stanley had thrown up all over Steve Klemp. "You did what?" He said that a few more times, only Stanley didn't know what to answer, on account of the nurse had just told him what had happened. Finally, Stanley's dad sat down in one of the chairs and shook his head. "Heck of a day," he'd said to no one in particular. "And just think, it's only the first day of school. The very first day."

Stanley didn't mind so much that all his dad did on the way home was yell at him. "Time is money," he said about three million times. "And I don't have enough of either to waste on foolishness. So listen up, buddy boy—it's a dog-eat-dog world out there, and you'd better get used to it. No more of this sensitive stomach nonsense! How're you ever going to get a job if you do things like . . . like . . ." He turned to look at Stanley. "What'd you do? Throw up on someone?" He rubbed the side of his head and sighed.

The truth was that no matter what the nurse had told his dad, throwing up on Steve Klemp was definitely not Stanley's fault. That was why he was practicing the Pledge of Allegiance, so that he wouldn't get the words mixed up like he had last year. Last year it was like all the words blended together, and when he sat down, Steve Klemp, who sat right in front of him, turned around and started laughing. Next, he told everyone nearby about how Stanley couldn't say the Pledge and how even an absolute zero could say the Pledge. Then he started saying how Stanley should say it again, right then, on account of everyone should be able to say the Pledge and anyone who couldn't probably wasn't a real American. Only instead of saying the Pledge again, Stanley had thrown up on him. The one and only

good thing about throwing up on Steve Klemp was
that for the rest of the year he never, not even once,
teased Stanley about how he said the Pledge of
Allegiance.

stanley's perfect year

On the morning of the first day of school Stanley's alarm clock worked perfectly. "Turn that off!" Jerry yelled, which Stanley immediately did. He jumped out of bed, noting that he was already a half hour ahead of schedule. Not only that, but this year he had convinced his mom to let him go with Robby Lanorsky to buy his school clothes, so he was sure to look cool. Usually, his mom liked to buy Stanley what she called "sophisticated outfits," which meant that Stanley looked like a miniature golfer. "And just what's wrong with that?" his mom had asked. "Golf is a very gentlemanly game. You should learn to play, Stanley." *Not this year,* he thought. This year he'd even had time to wash and dry his clothes fifteen times in a row, which was what Robby said was the very minimum before they would look cool. This year was going to be perfect, Stanley thought. Absolutely perfect!

When Stanley got to school, he went directly to his room. He knew that it was his room because he had the room number written down in three different places, and he checked all three, just to make sure. He was the first one to arrive, but a few minutes later other kids started coming over, standing around the door, waiting for the bell to ring. He even saw Theresa Wasnicki and waved to her—well, sort of waved. To his amazement, Theresa waved back! Another sign of a perfect year!

The new sixth-grade teacher hadn't yet arrived, so no one went inside. Usually, they knew ahead of time who the teacher was, but last year's sixth-grade teacher had gotten married during the summer and moved away. Stanley imagined that the new teacher would look just like Wendy the Counselor, and she would smile at them all and say, *This year, students, you may pick out your own seats.* That would be truly awesome! Stanley would go right to the very last seat in the last row, because even if it was going to be a perfect year, it was safest to sit where no one could see him.

Finally, the first bell rang and everyone went into the classroom, but there was still no teacher. After another minute, with everyone just standing around or sitting wherever they wanted to, Steve Klemp jumped up on his desk and shouted, "Everybody shut up! Since we got no teacher, I'm going to be in charge. Anyone got a problem with that?"

"Steven Albert Klemp, get down from there this very second!" a shrill voice said from the hallway door. Stanley couldn't see who had spoken, Steve Klemp was in his way. But he knew that voice. His stomach began to dance. "And now, boys and girls," the voice said as Steve Klemp climbed down, "please be so kind as to arrange yourselves in alphabetical order." And with that, Mrs. Olsen walked into the room.

As quickly as he could, Stanley checked the three places where he had his room number written down. Then he looked carefully around the room. Unless he'd made a mistake in all three places, and unless every single kid from last year had flunked, Mrs. Olsen was their new sixth-grade teacher. Stanley thought he might faint. He heard Mrs. Olsen slap her ruler against her desk. "Stanley Krakow! I believe you are familiar with alphabetical order, are you not? Why are you not in your proper seat?"

Mrs. Olsen loved alphabetical order, which meant

that just like the year before, Stanley would have to sit behind Steve Klemp. So much for a perfect year. But he could still have a great year, he thought. It was still possible. Maybe Mrs. Olsen was only a substitute. That was it, Stanley thought. Their real teacher was sick.

"Attention, please, children! Quiet! Miss Lundgren, last year's sixth-grade teacher, will not be returning this year. She was married in August and will live with her new husband on the East Coast. I have volunteered to be the new sixth-grade teacher. And if some of you don't do better than last year," she said, staring in Stanley's direction, "I'll be having you again next year! So shape up!"

All right, then, Stanley thought. *So much for having a great year.* But he could still have a good year. After all, he reasoned, he was still ready for anything. He stared at the back of Steve Klemp's head and then at Mrs. Olsen. Well, almost anything. And sure enough, when the class stood to say the Pledge of Allegiance, Stanley remembered all the words, and in the right order. He said his name perfectly too, which was what Mrs. Olsen had everyone in the class do before they got to sit back down. Then he opened his notebook to the first page of his reading section, which was to be their first-period subject. Mrs. Olsen even smiled at him because he already had a book cover for the reading book she was handing out. Yes, definitely a good year.

"And now, boys and girls, open to page one of your readers. From this day forward, for this Monday and for every Monday to follow until the end of the school year, we will have . . ." Mrs. Olsen paused, giving them her very best smile, which wasn't so easy with two rows of glued-in teeth. "Reading-aloud period!" Mrs. Olsen announced proudly.

No! Stanley wanted to shout. *Stop the world!* Where was the instant replay? Where was the referee? He wanted to demand a recount, a recall, anything! Stanley quickly counted how many kids were between him and Amelia Albrick, the first reader. Then he turned to the math section of his notebook, so that he could figure out how many minutes he had before it would be his turn. He looked at the clock, he added up the minutes, and he realized that he was doomed. He knew that although he had the best notebook in the class, with five pencils, five pens, a compass, a ruler, and covers for every one of his books, with his name and address already on them, this was not going to be a perfect year. Or even a great year. Not even a good one.

But wait! There was still Steve Klemp! Stanley

began to breathe again. When it came to reading, Steve Klemp was a force to be reckoned with. He was like the glaciers that they had studied the year before—nothing short of a nuclear blast could make him read quicker. Stanley wanted to lean forward and pat him on the back; he wanted to pat Mrs. Olsen on the back too, for always using alphabetical order. But then he counted the kids and the paragraphs, and he realized that despite all his plans and preparations, despite the slowest reader in the world sitting in front of him, he was truly sunk. Steve Klemp was going to have the shortest paragraph in the history of the world. Five words! And not one of them longer than two syllables!

Stanley closed his eyes and tried to imagine which would be worse: reading in front of the whole class or having his mom pick him up from the principal's office on the first day of sixth grade. Of course, he could always run into the street again and chance turning his brain into SpaghettiOs. Maybe his dad would take off another morning. Only his dad was still pretty mad about the bill he'd gotten from the hospital, so probably that wouldn't work so well. By the time Steve Klemp started his few words, Stanley's hands were wet and sticky, and he was breathing so fast that the edges of his vision started to blur.

"Next," Mrs. Olsen said. Stanley was about to tell her that he had a bathroom emergency, which never worked but was all he could think of, when someone begin to read. He opened his eyes and looked. In the last row Theresa Wasnicki had stood up and was busily wiggling her finger back and forth across the page, reading his paragraph perfectly and quickly. And Mrs. Olsen hadn't even looked up from her book! *Oh, thank you, God!* Stanley said to himself. *Thank you, thank you, thank you!*

"Hey, Mrs. Olsen!" Steve Klemp said. "Hey!"

Dear God, Stanley prayed, *please have Steve Klemp be quiet. Have his tongue fall off. You can put it back later. Please!*

"That's not Stanley reading, Mrs. Olsen. That's Theresa Wasnicki!"

Finally, Mrs. Olsen looked up. Stanley could hear Steve Klemp snickering. "Theresa," Mrs. Olsen asked, "why are you reading out of turn?"

"Because I like to read," Theresa answered without hesitation, "and Stanley hates to read. It makes him nervous, so why should he? And you," Theresa added, turning to Steve Klemp, "you're just mean, and first thing after school I'm going to teach you a lesson!"

"Theresa!" Mrs. Olsen said. "That will be quite enough! You apologize to Steven right now."

"Why?" Theresa asked. "He is mean, ask anyone. And if you make Stanley read, then you're mean too! Everybody knows he's a good reader."

"That will be enough!" Mrs. Olsen shouted.

"But it's the truth!"

"To the principal's office, young lady!"

"Wait." Stanley stood up, panting for breath. "Don't send her to the office. I'll read."

"You, young man, will read anyway!" Mrs. Olsen said, glaring at Stanley, her ruler gripped so tightly that her knuckles shone white. She turned to Theresa again and said, "And you will go to the principal's office. Now!"

Theresa didn't move, but she stared at Mrs. Olsen, who stared back. For a long moment Stanley waited for one of them to speak. It grew so quiet that Stanley could hear the squeak of desks as kids fidgeted for a better view.

"That's not fair!"

Stanley jumped at the words, as surprised as anyone that they had come out of his very own mouth. Mrs. Olsen turned away from Theresa, facing Stanley, her face reddening, her mouth working for words. Steve Klemp began to titter, then some of the other kids, too. Stanley felt everyone in the class watching him, but for once he didn't lower his eyes.

"Stanley Krakow," Mrs. Olsen said, "I will warn you once and once only—"

"I don't care what you say," he shouted. *"That's not fair!"*

Mrs. Olsen scribbled out notes for both of them, then came around her desk, ruler waving in her hand. "To the principal's office! *Now!*"

Walking down the hall toward the principal's office, Stanley stared at the floor, trying to hold back his tears. Next to him he heard an odd sound. He glanced over, just to make sure. Theresa was laughing.

"You sure did show them!" she said, slapping Stanley on the back hard enough to make him cough. "Boy, oh boy, you sure did!"

Stanley looked at her, his face puzzled. Theresa's dark eyes beamed, and a wide, happy smile lit her face. "Me?" he finally managed to say. He shook his head. "That was just a mistake," he said as they walked toward the principal's office. "I'm too afraid to talk in school."

Theresa smiled even more, her whole face laughing. "Of course you talk in school. What do you think we're doing right now?"

detention

Stanley and Theresa opened the heavy door to find Mr. Hardin, the principal, sitting behind his big desk. No-Pardon Hardin smiled brightly as the two of them entered; Stanley could have sworn that he actually licked his lips. "Mr. Krakow again, I see." He glanced at his watch. "It certainly didn't take you long to pay a visit. It appears that we begin the new year just where we left off. You are getting to be a regular juvenile delinquent! And you," he said, turning to Theresa. "You are . . . ?"

"Theresa Wasnicki. That's Wasnicki with an 's,' not a 'z.'"

"I know how to spell!" he thundered. "Let me see your notes."

They each handed him the notes Mrs. Olsen had written, explaining their offenses. Mr. Hardin stared at the pieces of paper, his head nodding and his fingers drumming the desktop.

"So, Mr. Krakow," he finally said, "you refuse to read." He looked up, frowning at Stanley, his thick eyebrows arching upward like exclamation points. "Reading, Mr. Krakow, is a time-honored American right. I suppose you don't care that men, good men, better men than you will ever grow up to be, have died to protect that right, a right that you now so flagrantly offend!"

"And women, too," Theresa added.

"What?" Mr. Hardin said, momentarily baffled.

"Women died to protect our rights too," Theresa answered. "Good women. And certainly better women than Stanley will ever grow up to be."

"Quiet!" Mr. Hardin boomed. "You're new here, Miss Wasnicki with an 's' and not a 'z,' so let me explain the rules. I talk, you listen! For every word I hear you utter, I will add ten minutes to your detention total. Is that understood?" Theresa nodded but said nothing. "Now, where was I? Oh, yes, young Krakow's refusal to read. If it were only possible, I would have

you whipped, Krakow—teach you the value of freedom. Unfortunately, that's against the law. So I'm
giving you two hours' detention this afternoon. And,
naturally, I'll inform your mother that you'll be late
coming home. Poor woman," he muttered, shaking
his head.

"And you." Mr. Hardin again turned to Theresa.
"Talking back to the teacher! And not just any teacher,
but one of our best! Well . . ." Mr. Hardin sighed
deeply, the fingers of his hands tapping together.
"Seeing as you haven't been sent in before," he finally
said, "I shall be lenient. One hour in detention. While
you sit in silence, young lady, think about the friends
you are making. I hope to see you hanging about with
a better class of student than Krakow here!"

For the rest of the day, Stanley worried about the
report Mr. Hardin would be putting into his file that
would follow him for the rest of his life. Un-
American! What college would accept him after reading that? He might not even get to go to highschool!
His life was going right down the drain, and all on
the very first day of school. After the final bell rang,
he slowly made his way to the detention room, where
he found Theresa already sitting quietly.

The detention room was next to Mr. Hardin's
office, and with the door open, which it always was,

Mr. Hardin could see every chair in the room. Also, there was no way to avoid hearing each and every word that Mr. Hardin was saying to his mom on the phone. "Yes, Mrs. Krakow," he started off, "I am sorry to be the one to inform you, but Stanley is once more in my care. . . . Indeed, I wish I did know what was wrong with him. . . . Yes, this is only the first day of school. Today the young man refused the all-American right of verbalizing the written word. . . . That is correct, Mrs. Krakow, reading. God only knows where this will lead, but he is quickly becoming a menace to the others in his class. In fact, today he incited one of our newer students to join with him in his subversive activities. . . . Yes, I would appreciate you speaking about this to him. Thank you, ma'am."

Mr. Hardin's next call was to Theresa's home. But he didn't say anything. "When will your mother be home, Miss Wasnicki?"

"She must've forgotten to fill me in on her plans," Theresa shot back.

From the other room, they heard Mr. Hardin laughing, which wasn't a pretty sound. "One extra hour of detention, Miss Wasnicki. Anything else you wish to add? No? Good. Now, let's try again. When can I contact your mother?"

Stanley heard Theresa sigh. "Do you have to call

her?" Theresa said. "Can't you just send a note home with me or something? She hates . . . you see, usually, I never get into trouble. Really, I don't, and I won't get into any more trouble either. I promise, I do." By the time she had finished, Theresa's voice had taken on a note of desperation that Stanley recognized from the hospital. "Only, please, Mr. Hardin . . . don't call her. Okay?"

"I hope you're taking notes, Krakow," the principal said, his voice floating in to them. "Young Miss Wasnicki shows repentance—a trait you might wish to acquire. Very well, Miss Wasnicki, I will take you at your word . . . this time. But be warned: Should I see you in here again, for any reason whatsoever, your parents will most definitely be involved. Are we clear?"

"Yes, Mr. Hardin," Theresa answered flatly.

"In that case, you can both leave after one full hour. Until then suffer in silence."

Normally, Stanley didn't mind being in detention. He excelled at not talking, and besides, it gave him plenty of time to draw maps of the lost world of Zambor. That day, though, he wanted only to put his head on the desk and cry. Theresa probably hated him by now, with everything Mr. Hardin had said. It was all his fault, of course; none of this would have happened if only he'd been brave enough to just stand up and read. *Stupid, stupid, stupid,* he said to himself, and with every "stupid," he knocked his forehead harder against the desktop.

Stanley felt something jab him in the arm. Glancing next to him, where Theresa sat, he saw her holding out a folded piece of paper. For a moment Stanley just stared at it, wondering whom Theresa wanted him to pass it to—there wasn't anyone else in the room. Suddenly, he realized the note must be for him, but even then, Stanley didn't reach out to take it. No one had ever before written a note to him. So Theresa let it fall onto his lap.

Very slowly, so that Mr. Hardin wouldn't notice or hear, he unfolded the paper and read, *I think you are VERY brave. Your friend, Theresa.* Stanley wasn't sure what he should do, so he just sat there, reading the note, again and again and again, making sure that it really said what it said. Also, he turned a deep shade of red.

He felt another jab against his arm. This time he took the note Theresa held out to him. It said, *What is your favorite color?* Stanley quietly got his notebook out, but then he paused, wondering what section he should use to answer. He didn't have a section for notes, only for subjects. At last he decided that a note about color was best taken from his art section. He wrote, *My favorite color is blue. What is your favorite color?* He carefully folded the note, then just as carefully unfolded it. He added, *Your friend, Stanley.*

The funny part was, until Theresa had asked, Stanley never even knew that he *had* a favorite color. And he certainly didn't know that he was her friend. But he was—it said so right there on the note. Just to be sure, he read it again: *Your friend, Theresa.* He carefully folded the first note and slipped it into his pocket, then, even more carefully, folded the note he'd just written and passed it to Theresa.

Theresa wrote back almost immediately. *I LOVE orange,* her note read. *Especially bright, bright orange! What's your favorite candy bar?*

Usually, no matter how many maps of Zambor Stanley drew, most of what he did in detention was worry about how much his mom would yell at him and about whether she would tell his dad, who would yell even more. But today, when the one-hour timer went off on Mr. Hardin's desk, Stanley realized he hadn't even thought about his parents. Stanley had been too busy thinking about colors and sounds and animals and movies. The truth was that no matter how much his parents yelled at him, he was sorry he couldn't do it all over again tomorrow. In class, with all the other kids there, Theresa would never send him a note, on account of everyone would make fun of her for sending a note to a total subzero wimpoid loser. She probably wouldn't talk to him either. But now he had a note, and that was all he needed. *Your friend, Theresa,* it said.

"Bye, Theresa," he said as they walked out of the detention room, again forgetting that he didn't like to talk. "See you later."

"Bye, Stanley," she said merrily, waving as she skipped away down the hall toward her locker. Stanley stood there, stupidly watching her go. Suddenly, he was aware of Mr. Hardin standing behind him.

"Loitering in the hall, are we, Mr. Krakow?" he asked snidely. Stanley didn't bother to answer. He smiled lamely and hurried outside.

On his way home Stanley took Theresa's note out of his pocket at every intersection, stopping to read it. He got home fifteen minutes later than he usually did after detention, but since his mom was mad already, she forgot to yell at him about it.

the invitation

Stanley stayed up until almost midnight that night thinking of questions Theresa might ask him the next time he saw her, then thinking of answers. What was his favorite holiday? What kind of dessert did he like best? Who was his favorite singer? It wasn't until the next morning that he realized he'd made it through the entire night without needing to visit the laundry hamper even once. He hadn't worried about if the window locks were screwed on tight enough or if alien space invaders had taken over Jerry's body. Or anything.

Stanley's plan for that morning was pretty simple: He would get to school forty-five minutes early. Who could tell? Theresa might also come early, and if not too many kids were around, she might even talk to him. At least, that's what he hoped. The one and only problem with his plan was that it didn't work. As Stanley waited outside the building more and more kids arrived for school, playing on the playground equipment, bouncing balls against the walls, or just sitting in front of classrooms. Theresa didn't arrive until just before the bell. Stanley saw her as soon as she walked through the playground gate, saw her look around, then walk straight toward him. "Hi!" she said. Stanley was so startled that he turned around to see who she was saying hi to—there was no one behind him.

"Silly." Theresa laughed. "Who do you think I'm talking to?" Stanley blushed and glanced around to see if anyone was watching. They were, only Theresa didn't seem to care. "Stanley," she said, "remember I told you about my aunt Helen? Well, she's flying here this weekend. So we can use the trampoline. But before that Aunt Helen invited me to her hotel for breakfast—want to come? She makes it right in her hotel room, so you don't need any money. She's a lot of fun," Theresa added when Stanley didn't answer.

"And I already asked her if it was all right if you came. And she already said yes."

Stanley wanted to pound his head on something. He'd stayed up half the night thinking of questions, and this wasn't one of them. Not only that, but kids were staring at them. He'd bet they were listening, too. Still, it wasn't a very hard question; all he had to do was answer yes or no. *Yes or no,* Stanley thought. *Yes or no.* Stanley looked up from the ground, smiling sheepishly. "Okay," he said. Then he remembered his manners. "Thanks."

Just then the bell for class rang, and everyone ran inside. Stanley gave a sigh of relief—he didn't know how many more questions he could answer before flubbing it. But just as quickly he began to worry. What time on Saturday? Where was Theresa's aunt's hotel? How would he get there? Theresa would probably forget to tell him, and Stanley knew he'd never be able to ask.

The girl in the row next to him poked Stanley in the arm. He wanted to tell her to go away, he had too much to think about to be bothered passing notes. The girl poked him again, whispering, "It's for you!"

Dumbly, Stanley took the note. Sure enough, right on the folded front of the paper was his name. In bright, bright orange. *Dear Stanley,* the note read once he'd unfolded it, *Please meet me at school at eight in the morning on Saturday. We can walk to my aunt's hotel from here, it's not very far. Your friend, Theresa.*

Stanley immediately stuck the note deep into his pocket so that he'd be sure not to lose it, but every two minutes he began to worry that maybe it had somehow disappeared, so he had to pull it out and check.

"Stanley!" Mrs. Olsen suddenly yelled at him, smacking her ruler against her desktop, "Stop fidgeting! If you have to go to the rest room, then go!" And even though Stanley didn't have to go, he went anyway, on account of it would be a whole lot more embarrassing if Mrs. Olsen discovered the note in his pocket and read it out loud, which was what she did with notes.

Once in the bathroom, locked inside a stall, Stanley took off one of his shoes and then the sock. He placed Theresa's note inside the sock, then put it and the shoe back on. Now no one could possibly find the note, and even though it itched quite a bit, at least he wouldn't spend all his time wondering if it had disappeared.

After the final bell Stanley ran the entire way home. "Mom!" he shouted, bursting in the front door. "I got invited to breakfast! This Saturday! I can go, right?"

He plopped onto one of the kitchen chairs and removed his shoe and sock, showing his mom the crumpled note.

His mom's mouth opened, then closed, then opened again, staring from the note to Stanley's shoe. "Why did you put the invitation in your shoe?" she finally asked.

"Mom. All I want to know is if I can go."

"Of course you can. Just make sure your room is spotless before you leave. Your dad and I have to go out Friday night, and I'm quite sure I do not want to get up Saturday morning to find a filthy room. Understood?"

Stanley at once ran to his room and began cleaning. He knew that he had three and a half days before breakfast with Theresa, but as his dad always said, better safe than sorry. Unfortunately, he forgot to put the note away, and Jerry picked it up off the TV as soon as he walked in.

"No!" Jerry chortled, holding the note. "It cannot be! The shrimp has a date! A date! So that's why you've been spending all that time in the bathroom. Practice, practice, practice!" Jerry laughed.

"Shut up! And give me that!" Stanley reached for the note, but Jerry held it up, waving it just above Stanley's grasping fingers. "I'm warning you!" Stanley shouted.

"What's the midget going to do? Puke on my shoes? What's—"

Just then Stanley punched him as hard as he could in the stomach, bending him double. "Ufff!" was all Jerry could say. The note fluttered to the floor. Stanley grabbed it and stuck it in his pocket.

He had never before hit his brother; he imagined that Jerry would now stuff a sock in his mouth so that no one could hear him screaming as he was beaten black and blue. To his surprise, all Jerry did once he was able to get up was say, "You could have just asked, you know." A little while later he added, "Good punch, by the way. Did I teach you that?"

Jerry pretty much left him alone after that, which was good, because Stanley had a ton of stuff to figure out before the end of the week, and he didn't think any of it would be in the *Encyclopædia Britannica*. First, he had to imagine all the things that either Theresa or her aunt might say to him, and then he had to think of how to respond. Stanley borrowed his mom's voice recorder, so that he could practice his answers. He practiced saying how good the breakfast was and how pretty the hotel looked and even what books he'd read and movies he'd seen, on account of that was what grown-ups usually liked to talk about.

"I don't know," Robby said as they sat on his porch

that Friday evening. "It could get hairy. You might need some reinforcements. Maybe you should take me along." Stanley's face scrunched up; he stared at his knees. "I'm only kidding!" Robby laughed. "Man, Stan, anyone ever tell you you're too serious? Hey, I know— let's walk down and see if the trampoline's set up! Maybe you can give your old buddy some pointers before we get going tomorrow."

They walked down to Theresa's house, but the gate was still locked. By walking to the end of the hedge and jumping, though, they could just see the side of the house. Sure enough, the trampoline had been laid flat, ready to use. But there was no sign of Theresa.

"You know her telephone number? Let's call her and see if we can practice."

Stanley realized that while he knew Theresa's favorite color, sound, city, and sport, she had never given him a telephone number. He shook his head.

"You don't have her number?" Robby jumped up again, glimpsing the trampoline. "Come on," he said, turning back toward his house. "Let's go look it up." As they walked Robby smiled shyly. "You might not believe this, Stan, but I've never been on a trampoline. Not one that big. My cousin has a little one, but nothing like that. I sure would like to practice before Jimmy and George see me."

The problem was "Wasnicki" wasn't in the phone book. Robby called information, but they didn't have a listing either. "Oh, well," Robby said. "Looks like I'll just have to fake it. Hey," he said, slapping Stanley on the back, "I know what we can do! Let's walk to the canyon, get some Poombah sticks, and scare the snakes! Great idea, those Poombah sticks. Maybe one day you'll take me when you go visit your uncle." Robby was already out the door and down the steps. "Come on!" he shouted back. "You don't want to be scaring snakes in the dark, do you?"

scrambled egg potato chips

After Stanley returned home from the canyon, he locked himself in the bathroom and reviewed all the questions and answers he'd taped on his mom's voice recorder, until Jerry flipped the lock open with a screwdriver. "Hey!" Stanley said, scrambling to pull his pants up. "You can't do that! I locked the door!"

Jerry smiled, tossing the screwdriver into the air and catching it as he walked in. "Can and did, squirt. Can and did. The rules state that it's perfectly acceptable to unlock the door if the current occupant is not in fact using the equipment." He moved over to the toilet, glancing down. "As, quite obviously, you are not."

"Rules?" Stanley repeated with a doubtful frown. "Really?

Jerry grinned. "And you thought you were the only one who knew any rules. So scram!"

Stanley sighed, then went into his room, laid out his clothes for the next day, set his alarm, and sat on his bed, wondering what else he could do. Nothing, there was nothing left. So he went over the questions he had thought of again, getting into bed early and pulling the blanket over his head so as to hear the tape recorder more clearly.

According to the chart in Stanley's pocket notebook, he had practiced questions and answers for over nine hours, and that didn't even count the times he'd fallen asleep with the tape recorder still running. Still, when Stanley woke up Saturday morning, the thought of talking to Theresa and her aunt made him want to run to the toilet and throw up. Stanley reached for the note under his pillow, smoothing it out and reading *Your friend, Theresa* over and over again, until his breathing returned to normal. He didn't think anyone would write *Your friend* as a joke.

Stanley got to the school playground nearly a half hour early, only to find Theresa already there, sitting on one of the swings and reading a book. "How come you're so early?" he said, coming up to her swing. When Theresa turned to him, Stanley noticed that her ear was all puffy and red. "What happened to your ear?" he added.

"What is this, an inquisition?" she shot back, frowning at him. "You're just as early, so answer your own stupid question."

Stanley just stood there, unable to think of anything. *Stupid, stupid, stupid!* he said to himself. *You're supposed to answer questions, not ask them!* "Uh," he finally said. "Well . . . I was scared that maybe you wouldn't be here or that I didn't remember the time right or maybe I got the day wrong," he blurted out all at once.

Theresa shrugged, then slowly smiled. "Okay, then. I'm just in a grumpy mood, that's all. My mom got into a fight with Aunt Helen last night, and then I got my ear whacked. On the trampoline," she added quickly. "I fell against the metal frame. Anyway," she said, hopping off the swing, "let's go."

After a few blocks of silence Theresa said, "You know what's fun? Picking out the best thing about each house we pass is fun. Want to play?" Stanley nodded, not having a clue as to what she was talking about. "Okay," Theresa said, "pick out what you like best about this house."

Stanley gazed at a house not much different from his own. "The door?" he guessed.

Theresa studied the door as they walked by. "A nice door. Okay, that's good. I also like the way the flowers line the walkway, especially the colors."

Stanley nodded. He hadn't really ever noticed the flowers, though he'd walked past this house a thousand times. He studied them more closely—they curved up the walkway like a rainbow, in the same pattern, first purple, blue and green, then yellow, orange, and red.

"Okay," Theresa went on, "how about this house?"

This time Stanley looked carefully. There weren't any flowers, but there was a gargantuan orange tree, with about a hundred oranges still on it. "The tree," he said.

Theresa beamed. "Yep, that's my favorite too."

They passed house after house, and they played until they came to a busy, commercial street. "That's my aunt's hotel," Theresa said, pointing at an old-fashioned building on the next block. "I hope she's still there," she added under her breath, then shrugged when she realized that Stanley had heard her. "My mom told Aunt Helen last night that if she didn't give her and my dad some more money, she might as well just pack up and leave, because she sure wasn't welcome." When Stanley looked puzzled, Theresa just smiled. "Some people are just like that. Go figure."

Aunt Helen turned out to be almost nothing at all like Theresa's mom. "Theresa and Stanley!" she said as the door swung open, as if she'd known Stanley forever. Then she gave both of them a hug. Stanley wasn't so sure about that part, but inside the hotel room—which was really two rooms and a kitchen—Aunt Helen had gifts for them both. Theresa got a sweatshirt with the words BEST NIECE IN THE WORLD on it, and Stanley got a Dodgers baseball cap, which more than made up for the hug.

They went into the kitchen, where Aunt Helen had them sit at a table surrounded by windows looking out at the hotel's flower garden. "And now," Aunt Helen announced, "Theresa's favorite breakfast! Scrambled eggs!"

Stanley did his very best to smile, only the thing was, scrambled eggs usually made him sick. His mom always left some of it runny, and even though Stanley was careful to not eat those parts, even looking at them made his stomach turn over. Given a choice, he'd rather eat Camp Hayseed lumpy cereal than scrambled eggs. "Of course, scrambled eggs wouldn't be Theresa's favorite breakfast without these," Aunt Helen went on. She pulled a bag of potato chips onto the counter.

Again, Stanley tried to smile, only he had no idea

of what was going on. What were the potato chips for? To hide the runny parts? He watched Aunt Helen whip a bowl of eggs with a fork, then pour them into a frying pan. Stanley heard the eggs sizzling, then Aunt Helen dumped the entire bag of potato chips into the pan and stirred them in too.

"Scrambled egg potato chips!" Theresa announced proudly, poking Stanley in the arm. "It's my very own invention. Doesn't it look great?" she said as plates appeared before them.

He took a bite, but not a large one, then nodded vigorously. Scrambled egg potato chips tasted great! And not a runny bit to be seen! Just wait until he told Robby! Robby's mom could make them. Jerry could make them. Why, maybe even he could make them. After all, it looked simple enough.

"Want some more?" Aunt Helen asked. They both nodded. Scrambled egg potato chips!

Theresa and Stanley were just about to go into the living room and watch TV when the phone rang. "Hello, Marge," Aunt Helen said into the receiver. Theresa plopped back into her chair, saying something under her breath and kicking at the leg of the table. "Marge, I don't think that's such a good idea right now. How about giving her the rest of the morning?" Stanley could hear the other person shouting at Aunt

Helen, but all Aunt Helen said was, "Well, Marge, she's always welcome to come and visit. And so are you." Then she held the phone out to Theresa. "Your mother wants to talk to you."

Theresa took the phone. "Hello," she said. Then she just listened, kicking the table leg harder and harder. "Okay," she finally said. She got up, putting the phone back in its cradle. "I have to go home," she told them, blinking back her tears. "My mom and dad are taking me to the movies, so I have to go home now and get ready."

Aunt Helen gave her another big hug and said, "I love you, honey, don't forget that." Then she shook hands with Stanley and told him what a pleasure it had been to meet him.

On the way back home Stanley wanted to ask Theresa why she'd lied about what her mother had said. Her mother had been yelling so loud that even if Stanley had stuffed napkins in his ears, he would have heard every word. And no one ever mentioned going to the movies.

Theresa walked quickly, not bothering to even glance at the houses they passed. Stanley wanted to say something to make her feel better. But what? What? It was easier to just keep quiet.

Finally, he turned to her. "You ever kick rocks?" he

blurted out, then looked down at the ground, turning red. Lame! "What I mean," Stanley said, forcing his head back up, "is that I can teach you the official rules of Rock Kicking, if you want." When Theresa didn't answer, he added, "It's a real sport."

"Well," she said. "Will it take long? My mom will probably kill me already. I can't get home too late."

"Nah," Stanley said. "Sometimes I even get home quicker, on account of the crowd cheering . . ." Stanley's mouth dropped open, realizing what he'd said. "Not a real crowd," he stammered. "But, you know, uh . . ."

"Sure, I know," Theresa said, smiling for the first time since the phone call. "Let's play."

As they walked Stanley showed Theresa the best type of rocks to pick and explained the rules. Theresa was a natural—her very first kick was twenty-eight steps, and it stopped right in the middle of the side- walk. By the time they got to the beginning of Theresa's block, she was skipping her kicks perfectly from the sidewalk into the street and back again. In fact, Stanley looked around, hoping that the ESPN van was filming it all. He hadn't told Theresa about the ESPN van—he wasn't *that* brave.

"That was fun, Stanley," Theresa said. "Only I think we'd better quit here. I think I'd better walk the rest of the way alone. My mom doesn't know you went with me."

"Wait!" Stanley practically shouted as she walked away. When Theresa turned back, Stanley dug a small box out of his pocket and held it out to her. His mom was always lecturing him about manners and being polite, so Stanley had bought Theresa a gift, on account of she'd invited him for breakfast. "It's for you," he said.

There was a green rubber band around the box. Slowly, Theresa slid it off and removed the top. Inside was a pair of shoelaces, which Stanley was afraid might be a truly all-time, world-record bozo gift. Only these shoelaces were bright, bright orange.

"They glow in the dark," Stanley added when Theresa didn't say anything.

Theresa stared at them for a long while. "Thank you, Stanley," she said without looking up from the gift. "I like them, I do." Her smile seemed to quiver as she stared at them; she ran a finger slowly down and up the box. "I'll wear them to school on Monday." Then she turned, running toward her house.

uncle willie's last story

Robby and George beat one side of the bushes with their Poombah sticks, shouting "Poombah! Poombah!" with every blow, while Stanley beat the other side. Jimmy walked behind Stanley, watching the bushes carefully. "Whose idea was this, anyway?" he asked again. "I mean, guys, you're listening to a man who they won't let out of the hospital. How much sense does that make?" When none of the others even paused, he added, "'Poombah' is not even an American word. You think American snakes understand? Come on, you guys, in American, 'Poombah' might mean 'attack.'"

"Poombah! Poombah!" Robby shouted. Then, "Good question, Jimmy. Really. We'll ask him when we get there. If we survive," he added, swinging his Poombah stick and shouting again.

It wasn't often that Stanley got to lead the way, but after they'd climbed up out of the canyon, the others didn't even ask, but just walked behind him. Stanley didn't stop at the hospital's reception desk, but headed directly for the men's room, trying not to think about Robby, George, and Jimmy following behind or what Uncle Alan would do once he saw them all. He was still at the same hospital—for now, at least, his mom had said. But what if he didn't recognize Stanley? Worse, what if he decided to adopt Robby, George, and Jimmy? Stanley was beginning to wish that he'd never told Robby about Poombah sticks.

As usual, Stanley had worried about all the wrong things, because when they got to the visiting room, Uncle Alan was nowhere to be seen. "I thought you said he was out here all the time," Jimmy griped. Stanley just shrugged, staring around the room once again, as if maybe he'd overlooked someone. For the first time he realized that he had never actually been to his uncle's room and didn't know where it was.

"You seen the guy who tells stories?" Stanley asked a man in a wheelchair. Both of his legs were in casts.

"Oh," the man said, his face brightening, "you mean Alan . . . Alan Ladd." Then his face dropped again. "No. He's not allowed out of his room anymore."

"Why?" Stanley asked.

"He keeps trying to leave. Says there's nothing left for him to recover from." The man started poking at one of his casts. "Itches like crazy," he said. He rubbed his hands together, faster and faster, then placed them palm down on the part of his cast that had been itching. "Ah!" He smiled. "It's the heat, stops the itching. A trick Alan showed me. Good man, that Alan."

Stanley felt an elbow in his back—Robby hissing at him to go on. "So," Stanley said, trying to seem unconcerned, "what room's he in? Alan?"

"Room 315," the man answered. "Just down the hall. But you can't visit him."

"Straitjacket?" Robby put in hopefully. "Armed guards?"

The man laughed. "No, not quite. It's that they took his street clothes away, and he doesn't much care for the color of the bathrobe they gave him. Won't allow visitors in now. Otherwise, that's where most of us would be. He's a card, no mistake about it."

Stanley nodded, then turned toward the hall. The others followed close behind. At room 315 they paused. "Plan?" Robby asked.

For a moment no one moved or spoke. Jimmy scrunched up his face, then pointed at the doorknob. "Go in?" he said. Stanley nodded, swinging the door open.

Inside, Uncle Alan was reading a newspaper, his back toward them. "Oh," he said when he finally glanced over his shoulder, "I thought it was the nurse. Better by far, though not as good looking! Nephew Stanley! And friends, I presume?" Stanley introduced Robby, George, and Jimmy. "Charmed, I'm sure," Uncle Alan said, standing and turning to them, shaking each of their hands. "And just in time. Rumor has it that I will be shipped off to a more, uh, secure institution. But I'm sure that is not the purpose of your visit—unless you've smuggled in clothes of my approximate size?" All four shook their heads at once. "No, I didn't think as much. Then, what?"

"Poombah sticks," Jimmy said bluntly. "How do we know that snakes in this country understand Madagascan?"

"Ah, yes," Uncle Alan said, pulling his bathrobe a bit tighter around him. "Please excuse my attire, gentlemen—I would not usually entertain you thusly dressed. Seeing that it is a life-and-death situation, though . . ." He nodded his head, thinking, then looked up again. "I believe I understand the young man's problem. He's confusing snake capacities with human capacities. Humans use sound, while snakes use . . ." Uncle Alan opened his mouth, letting his tongue wiggle around. "Their tongues! They taste the world around them, not just flavors, as we do, but movement, feelings, sensations of all kinds. 'Poombah' doesn't mean anything to anybody but a snake—the word moves the air and, together with a certain vibration that the stick produces when striking the ground, fills the snake with unimaginable terror. Ah," he said, looking down at the four blank faces, "I believe a story would convey my point more fully. Shall we?"

There were two beds in the room. Uncle Alan had the four of them all sit on one bed. Then he began. "Stanley has no doubt told you of my adventures in Madagascar. However, that was not the end of my need to learn about snakes. Indeed not! For some years later, as I was wandering around the wilds of Mexico, searching for the lost gold of the Aztecs, I had the misfortune of finding it. Beautiful face masks, almost life-size animals, bows and arrows—all of pure gold! And all guarded by hundreds, even thousands of deadly snakes!

"I wish I could tell you that it was by my great skill that I located this vast fortune, but, alas, that would not be quite true. The local natives, a bit peeved that I was having a long run of good luck at the poker table, decided that they might regain their losses by tossing me into a deep cavern. It was there that I discovered the gold. And the snakes. 'Poombah!' I shouted. They backed away a bit but did not leave. I had no Poombah stick, of course, that was the problem. And no way of getting one. Time to increase my snake vocabulary, I decided. And quick! The Aztecs had once sacrificed humans to these very snakes. But the Aztecs had been dead and gone for over four hundred years, and the snakes were getting a touch hungry. I ask you, boys— have you ever seen a snake smile? Up close and personal? Well, I have!"

mr. hardin's encore performance

"Did you ever see a snake smile?" Jimmy asked Monday morning as they all waited for the first bell of school. "Up close and personal?" Half a dozen of his classmates eagerly shook their heads, eyes widening. "Well, I have!"

Stanley only half listened to Jimmy tell about their walk back through the canyon and the many deadly snakes they had escaped. He just couldn't stop thinking about Theresa, about whether she would actually wear the orange shoelaces to school. If she did wear them, would she tell everyone they were a gift from

Stanley? And would that be the positively most horrible thing that had ever happened to him in his life? Or the most wonderful? Stanley couldn't quite figure it out, and he didn't get a chance to, either, for Theresa was absent. Nor was she in school on Tuesday or Wednesday or Thursday.

When Friday came and Theresa still wasn't in school, Stanley decided he couldn't wait any longer. He'd already spent most of his afternoons walking up and down past Theresa's house, hoping to see her. The trampoline had been tilted up against the house again, but no one had bothered to wrap it in its cover. The place looked so quiet, it could have been deserted. Maybe it was, Stanley thought. Maybe Theresa's parents had moved, and he would never see her again, not even to say good-bye. Stanley *had* to find out; he just *had* get her phone number.

When the lunch bell sounded that Friday, and every other kid in his class was laughing and hurrying for the playground door, Stanley made his way quietly in the opposite direction of the classroom. The cloakroom was empty this time of year, except for the three emergency coats that Mrs. Olsen kept hung neatly in a corner. Stanley sat noiselessly beneath them, not daring to even open his lunch bag. Waiting. Finally, he heard Mrs. Olsen's heavy footsteps moving toward the hallway door and then the door closing behind her.

Stanley peeked out, carefully checking the classroom for enemy activity or spies at the windows. The place was clear. Even so, he crept on his knees, head down, all the way to Mrs. Olsen's desk, where he slowly and carefully pulled open the drawer marked FILES. At that point he had to stop, breathing deeply to calm his shaking hands—something real heroes never had to do, he suspected. At least, he'd never heard any of the cowboys on *Cowboy Roundup* talk about it. Stanley forced himself back into the files, flipping through them until he got to the one labeled WASNICKI. He looked, looked again, and looked a third time just to be sure. There was no phone number! *To be supplied* was all anyone had bothered to write.

Stanley slammed the drawer shut, then dived under the desk when he realized how much noise he'd made. But no one noticed, no one came into the room to investigate, and after a few minutes Stanley crawled back to the cloakroom, where he ate his lunch. He just had to get her phone number! He had to! But how? There was nothing more he could do. He was lucky he hadn't been sent to the principal's office already.

The principal's office! Of course! Stanley nearly choked on his peanut butter and jelly sandwich. Mr.

Hardin would have Theresa's phone number, wouldn't he? Sure he would, because when he and Theresa had been in detention, Mr. Hardin had called Theresa's home. And the number would be locked in the huge file cabinet in the principal's office. And Stanley had the set of backup keys!

Or did he? It had been last year, after all. He had put them away, he remembered that much. But where? And were they still there? And would they work even if he did find them? And even if they did work, how was he going to get into Mr. Hardin's office?

Questions buzzed at him like flies; it was all Stanley could do to sit in his seat that afternoon. When the final bell rang, he was first out the door, pushing larger and stronger kids out of his way. He even pushed Steve Klemp out of his way. Then he ran the entire twelve blocks to his home, not even pausing to see if ESPN was filming.

The key ring he'd found in Mr. Hardin's office was right where he remembered leaving it, in a pair of brown church socks that he never wore and that also hid his two favorite marbles, an Indian-head penny, and an authentic shark's tooth. Stanley grabbed the keys, then ran back out of the house, looking for Robby. But Robby had already left for soccer practice.

There wasn't any choice. Not really. After all, if

Robby wasn't in school, even for a day, wouldn't he call and find out why? And for sure, Robby would call if he was absent. Stanley was Theresa's only friend; he just had to check on her. Which meant that he just had to get her number. No matter what. Stanley turned back toward school, stuffed his hands into his pockets, and started walking as quickly as he could.

The playground was completely deserted by the time Stanley got there, but he could hear the janitor inside the building, buffing the floors. Stanley found the door farthest from the hum of the janitor's buffer and pushed in. He walked slowly, keeping to the shadows, but even then, his sneakers squeaked against the newly waxed floor, alerting the world to his presence. *Well,* Stanley thought, *it isn't against the law for a kid to be in school after school is over, is it?* Actually, he didn't know. Then he had another terrible thought: What if Mr. Hardin was still in his office? He would knock, that's what he would do; and if Mr. Hardin was there, Stanley would say that he just came by to apologize for all the trouble he'd caused. That would probably be enough to make Mr. Hardin pass out cold.

All Stanley's worries were for nothing, of course. It was Friday, and Mr. Hardin had hurried home to get himself ready for a big night out. No one answered Stanley's knock; no one yelled at him when he turned the knob, swinging the door open. The office was empty and quiet. *Too quiet,* Stanley thought as he closed the door behind him. The noise of the keys coming out of his pocket echoed off the walls. He nearly dropped the ring trying to fit the first key into the lock of the drawer labeled 5TH–6TH GRADE. It was the wrong key, anyway, and worse than that, it stuck when he tried to pull it out, coming away only with a yank that sent Stanley flying across the room, bouncing on his bottom a couple of times. He got up and tried again with another key. Same thing, but this time he bounced only once.

Finally, on the third try, the lock clicked open. Stanley slipped the file marked WASNICKI out of the drawer. Down the hall he could hear the janitor's buffing machine cough and then go silent. It was followed by a sound far, far more frightening—singing! And not any singing either, but the worst singing in the world! Without a sound, Stanley slid the file drawer closed, then shoved Theresa's file under his shirt. He looked around for a place to hide, but there wasn't any.

Just as the door to Mr. Hardin's office began to creak open, Stanley ducked into the detention room. There was still no place to hide, but at least it was dark and windowless. Stanley moved against the wall, felt coats hanging from a long coatrack. He remembered that he'd lost a coat last winter and wondered if it was one of the ones he was leaning against. Not exactly the best time to check it out, Stanley figured. He moved to the end of the coatrack, placing a coat over his head as the singing came nearer.

To Stanley's horror, the singing didn't stay in Mr. Hardin's office, but moved steadily toward the detention room. Stanley held his breath. At least the lights didn't come on. But then Stanley remembered Mrs. Olsen's lesson on bats, how they located their prey with sonar squeaks. Maybe Mr. Hardin used his singing in the same way. Sure enough, Stanley heard the first coat being lifted up, then set back. *He knows that someone's in the coats!* Stanley thought. *He just doesn't know where!* The second coat was lifted up, then set back. Then the third coat. There was only one coat left before the one under which Stanley was hidden. "Aha!" Mr. Hardin practically screeched. Stanley cringed, then he heard the sound of the coat being put on. "What woman can resist leather?" Mr. Hardin said with a chuckle, patting the coat. "I am set!"

Stanley waited until he heard the office door close before he spewed out the air in his lungs. A definite record. For once, though, he was glad there were no hidden cameras. Noiselessly, he made his way back into the office, and after copying Theresa's phone number into his pocket notebook, he reopened the file cabinet and returned Theresa's file to its place. As carefully as he could, Stanley opened the door, then squeaked down the hall and out of the building. He had to use the rest room something terrible, but he didn't stop. Even after he'd closed his own front door behind him, he didn't feel safe, but kept peeking out the windows, expecting a cop car to pull up, lights flashing. But no one came to bother him.

that's what sidekicks are for

"Wow!" Robby said after listening to Stanley's story. He was sitting on his bed. Stanley sat on the spare bed opposite him. "This is way past Zamborific. I don't know . . . we might have to discover a whole new planet for this!"

Stanley lifted his shoulders, then let them drop. "I guess," he said. He couldn't stop thinking about Theresa's mom saying that if Theresa wasn't more careful, next time she might fall out a window. What if the next time had come? After all, she'd been out of school a whole week.

"So we call her," Robby said, bounding off the bed. "Ask her what the deal is." When Stanley didn't move, Robby shook his head, squinting. "What?" he said.

"Well . . ." Stanley forced himself to lift his head. "We're not supposed to have her phone number, right? What if we call and it's not Theresa who answers? We could just be getting her in more trouble."

"Right! Good thinking, Stan! Like, what if the reason she hasn't been in school is that she's been kidnapped and the kidnappers are holding the whole family in the cellar?"

"I don't think they have a cellar," Stanley put in. "Nobody has a cellar around here."

"So big deal, they're tied up in the closet!" Robby said. "The point is, we need to be careful! Not give ourselves away! Hey, I know!" He ran to his closet, digging through a pile of tangled objects thrown into a corner. "Got it!" he said, pulling out a plastic bullhorn. "Remember this? It changes your voice. It's got one button that makes you sound like a grumpy old man. We'll use this, pretend to be, I don't know, how about bill collectors?"

"I don't think anyone's going to be too happy to get a call from a bill collector."

"Right," Robby said. "Okay, then, a fund-raiser. My mom's always getting calls asking her to donate money to somebody. Who knows, maybe the kidnappers will donate? That would be cool! Besides," he said, "it's just to see who answers the phone. If it's Theresa, you forget the phony voice and just talk to her."

Stanley felt his heart suddenly begin to race. "What do you mean, me?" he peeped, unable to get his voice right. "It's your idea, you talk to her!"

Robby just shook his head. "Against the rules, Stan. There's only one hero in each movie. And you're it. When the action starts, you're the one the camera focuses on. I'm just the sidekick, the faithful companion." He picked up the phone. "I dial the number," he said as he dialed, "because that's my job." Then he handed it to Stanley, along with the bullhorn. "But you do the talking."

As it turned out, the bullhorn wasn't necessary; Theresa answered the phone herself. "Uh, h-h-hello," Stanley stammered.

"Your name!" Robby hissed. "Tell her who's calling!"

"Oh, right! Hi, this is Stanley. Remember, I came over to your aunt's—"

"Stanley, I know who you are," Theresa said, a little grumpily. "How'd you get our number? No one's supposed to have it."

For a moment Stanley said nothing. He thought it

was probably a good time to hang up, but the words just burst out of him. "I was worried about you," he said. "I wanted to find out if you were all right; you've been gone a whole week." When Theresa didn't answer, Stanley said, "Are you? All right, I mean?" Still, there was only silence on the phone. "Theresa?"

"I . . . I'm not allowed to talk on the phone," she said. "If my mom hears me, she'll . . . well, it'll be even worse, that's all." Her voice was shaking, the way Stanley's did in reading-aloud period. "Thanks for thinking about me, but you don't have to. I'm okay. Only don't call anymore. Okay, Stanley? Really, don't. It's bad enough already."

"But what's wrong?" Stanley asked. "Maybe I can help."

Again, there was a long silence. "Thanks for the shoelaces," Theresa finally said. "I look at them at night, when I'm in bed. They glow, you know." And then another long pause—Stanley thought he might have heard Theresa crying, but he wasn't sure. "Goodbye," she finally said. The phone clicked, then went dead.

"What'd she say?" Robby asked. "Come on, Stan! What's the story?"

So Stanley told him the story.

"Wow!" Robbie said when Stanley had finished.

"Wow, what?" Stanley asked.

"This is hero stuff for sure!" Robby announced. "No doubt about it. They couldn't have written the script any better!" Stanley stared at him like he was crazy. "Don't you get it, Stan? Don't you see? Theresa's the lady in distress; she's managed to smuggle out a note."

"What note?" Stanley interrupted.

"Note, phone call, whatever," Robby said, waving a hand. "The point is, she's in trouble and you have to save her. You have to rescue her. That's what heroes do."

Stanley's face scrunched up—his nose wrinkled and his lips puckered. "Robby," he said, "I'm not a hero. Okay? I mean, think about it. Think about me!"

"Well . . ." Robby sighed. "You have a point. But . . . no, no, I'm on to you!" he practically shouted. "I got you! This is exactly what heroes always do! Try to convince everyone that they're not really heroes."

"But I'm *not* a hero!" Stanley protested.

"That's not up to you," Robby shot back. "Why'd Theresa tell you she was in trouble? So you could do nothing? Sure, that's just what she was thinking: 'I'll tell my good friend Stanley I'm in trouble, because I know he won't do a thing.' Man, Stan, remind me to call someone else if I'm ever in a fix!"

Stanley kicked at the carpet, hoping that Robby would just disappear. Fat chance, since it was Robby's room. "Okay," Stanley finally said. "But you're going with me!"

"Of course!" Robby beamed. "I'm the sidekick. I can't possibly stay behind! So what's the plan?" he asked, tumbling back onto his bed. When Stanley didn't answer, he sat up, frowning. "You do have a plan, don't you? Well, don't you?"

plans

"So I need a plan," Stanley told his uncle after explaining what had happened. "And quick. Robby's parents are going out and I'm sleeping over— so tonight's the night."

Uncle Alan stared out the window, hardly seeming to notice Stanley. He'd been writing letters when Stanley came in, but now the paper and pen were lying forgotten on his lap. "Nice view, isn't it? I'll miss it," he said with a sigh. Then he turned toward Stanley. "Like my new bathrobe?" he asked. It was thick and long. "A going-away present from some of the fellows on the floor. I don't suppose I'll have much of a view where I'm going. I hear they have bars on the windows. Maybe I can tunnel out. Did I ever tell you about the time I was jailed in Singapore?"

Stanley was beginning to panic. "I need help, Uncle Alan!" He glanced at his watch; he had to be back at Robby's house in less than an hour. "And I need it now!"

For a minute Stanley thought that his uncle might be angry with him, because he didn't speak, but just sat there, pulling at his chin. But then he smiled. "Stanley, I do believe I'm growing to like you more with every visit. Yes, of course you need a plan. Unfortunately, the only one who can come up with that plan is you. Ah, ah, ah," he said when Stanley started to complain, "I'll help, don't worry. The first thing you need is a list of skills—what you're good at."

"But I'm not good at anything," Stanley moaned.

"We all think that from time to time . . . which is where I come in. It's quite amazing, really, how many fine qualities can be uncovered when you sit down with a good listener. And I, my friend, am a very good listener. So," Uncle Alan said, sitting back in his chair and putting his letter-writing paper onto the table next to him, "tell me everything you like to do. Leave out nothing!"

So Stanley began talking. He told his uncle about rock kicking and bush jumping, about holding his breath and reading the encyclopedia, and even about the lampshade game. He told him everything. When he was finally finished, his uncle said nothing at first, but he carefully studied the list he had made.

"Well!" he said at last. "This is certainly a unique list of talents! All we need to do is match them to the task at hand." Uncle Alan sat up, winking at Stanley. "That, my friend, is the easy part! Now, what you need isn't a plan, exactly, but a whole bunch of plans, because you never quite know what's going to happen. And that's what we're going to come up with, so that whatever happens, you'll be ready. Now, I know you told me the story once, but tell me again. And this time don't leave out a thing!"

As Stanley talked his uncle jotted down notes. Stanley told him about the old house that the Wasnicki family had moved into and how he'd seen Theresa cutting the grass. He told him about the hospital, about all the times Theresa had saved his life, and even about going to the hotel with Theresa's aunt Helen, who was rich and who'd flown in all the way from . . . Stanley couldn't remember what city Theresa's aunt was from, but Uncle Alan said that even details like that might be important. "Denver," Stanley

finally said, a bit unsure. "Yeah, Denver, on account of
Theresa said she was as rich as the Denver mint." He
gave his uncle as complete a rundown of the house and
grounds as possible, including the hole he'd dug under
the fence.

Uncle Alan kept his head down as Stanley spoke,
busily circling certain of Stanley's talents while cross-
ing out others, moving them into columns labeled
Plan A, Plan B, and so on. Fifteen minutes later they
were done. "Wow," Stanley said when they went over
the plans, "that *was* easy."

"The hard part is getting it done, my friend." Uncle
Alan handed the plans over to Stanley, then settled
back again, staring out the window. "Yes, sir." He
sighed. "I'm sure going to miss the view."

"So," Stanley asked after the quiet had returned to
the room, "what's your plan?"

Uncle Alan looked puzzled. "Say again?" he said.

"Your plan. What're you planning for your escape?"

"Well . . ." Uncle Alan shrugged. "Not quite as ele-
gant as yours, I'm afraid." He winked, then said in a
whisper, "I lack your talents." Slowly, his smile faded.
He sighed once more. "I don't have much of a choice,
really," he said. "I can't stay Uncle Alan and stay here."

"But why do you have to stay Uncle Alan at all?"

"I've been over this with your mom and the doctors

and who knows who else. I like being Alan Ladd!" he said, slapping the table. "It's who I am, who I really am. I don't care where they send me or how long I have to stay; I won't go back to being someone I don't like. Someone I was never meant to be! I simply won't!"

"I don't get the problem," was all Stanley said. But his uncle had gone back to staring out the window, his jaw set, muttering to himself. "Listen, Uncle Alan," Stanley forced himself to say. "Just listen, okay?" When his uncle turned to him, Stanley took a deep breath and began. "Robby calls me Stan, and my mom calls me Stanley, and my dad calls me buddy boy—but I'm still the same person, aren't I? Like, remember when you adopted me?" Stanley took a piece of paper out of his back pocket, carefully unfolding it. "'I, Alan Ladd, do hereby and forthwith officially adopt Stanley Uriah Krakow as my nephew,'" Stanley read. "So why can't you officially adopt a new name? Why can't you change your name from Alan Ladd to Willie . . ." He had to think a bit to remember his uncle's old last name. "Willie Burns. If your new name's the same as your old name, that doesn't mean you have to act like your old self, does it? I mean, isn't that the only thing people are worried about? What you call yourself? If you called yourself Uncle Willie, couldn't you still act like Uncle Alan?"

Uncle Alan started to say something, but nothing came out, so he closed his mouth. "Did we put 'genius' on that list of your talents, Stanley?" he finally managed to say. Then he looked at his watch. "You'd better get home." He smiled brightly. "There are plans to ready! Action to take! Go, then! And may success follow in your footsteps!"

the rescue

"Have fun," Robby said as his mom stepped toward the door, his smile as wide and eager as the kid's in the toothpaste commercial. Stanley moved back even farther into the shadows of the Lanorskys' front hall, biting nervously at his lip. Robby never smiled like that; it should have been a dead giveaway. If Stanley or Jerry ever tried a smile like that, they would've been put on restriction just for what they were thinking.

But all Mrs. Lanorsky did was bend down to give Robby a kiss. "Remember," she said, "your dad and I are trusting you to keep the house clean. Are we clear about that?"

Robby beamed his toothpaste smile at her again—Stanley wanted to vomit. "Crystal," he replied. "It'll be like we weren't even here." She gave him a smile and another kiss, then closed the door behind her, walking down the steps to where Mr. Lanorsky had the car waiting.

Robby turned to Stanley, grinning. He held up a finger to his lips and tiptoed toward his room, motioning for Stanley to follow him—as if anyone cared what they were doing. The only other person in the house was Robby's older brother, Charles, and he was busy with the box of Alvin Bagley's old issues of *Playboy* that he had dumped in the trash so that Charles could find them. He'd stay locked in his room for hours—that was, if he ever came out. That many *Playboy*s might kill him.

Back in Robby's room they began to dress. Stanley handed Robby a Dark Man hood, then took out the dark pants and dark shirt that he'd brought over in his pajama bag, putting them on.

"You sure this is necessary?" Robby said, holding the mask in front of him. "I mean, what if someone sees us?"

"That's the whole point," Stanley told him. He

slipped on his mask, then pulled Robby over to the closet mirror. "Look." Then he turned off the lights.

Stanley was no more than an inky blur in the mirror, while Robby's white face floated in the darkness like the head of a ghost. "Zamborific!" Robby crowed, slipping on his own Dark Man hood. "I will never again doubt the fantastic and impenetrable mind of Stanley Krakow, Boy Genius!"

Outside it was quiet, the only noise being a muffled drone coming from the TVs inside people's houses. Without speaking, Robby motioned toward a tree two doors down. Silently, they dashed for it, then paused while Robby consulted the map Stanley had drawn, showing all the possible routes to Theresa's house and all the places they could hide along the way. Four to six blocks, depending on which streets they took. "Okay," Robby whispered, "two houses up, Mrs. Garcia's rose-bushes. Ready?"

They made the first two blocks before even seeing a car, but that one swung around the corner so fast that it nearly caught them. Robby dived into a flower-bed, pulling Stanley with him.

"Close," Robby whispered once the car had passed. "We'd better stay low." He started across the lawn on his belly. Stanley wanted to tell him that two kids dressed all in black crawling across someone's front yard probably looked a lot more suspicious than two kids just walking, but all he did was follow along, trying his best not to get grass stains on the knees of his pants. His mom was always telling him not to get grass stains on his clothes.

It took them almost thirty minutes, which included avoiding three more cars, one dog, and two kids from school who were out late, before they came to Theresa's block. Robby whispered, "Okay, final-approach pattern. Team leader will now address his troops." When all Stanley did was look around, Robby poked him. "Team leader," he repeated. "That's you."

"Oh," Stanley said. "Right." Under his hood he felt his face reddening. Another good reason for superheroes to wear masks. "Well . . . just follow me," he finally said, then ran across the street in a crouch, hoping and praying that he wouldn't trip. He headed toward the side of the Wasnickis' yard, to where he had dug the hole under the fence. Some leaves had blown into it, but it was still usable. Stanley pushed the leaves away and scurried under, hiding behind the big bush on the other side.

"Cool," Robby said under his breath as he came up beside Stanley. "Just what I would have expected of a boy genius."

Stanley peeked out at the house, but no lights were

on. At least, none that they could see. But what did that mean? The plan was to get onto the porch roof, the same one that Theresa had used to get from her room to the yard. Only what was the sense of that if Theresa was downstairs? And what about Mrs. Wasnicki? It sure would be good to find out just where she might be.

"Follow me," Stanley said, dashing for the side of the house. Robby beat him by five feet, but the important thing was that no one had shouted at them, no lights had come on, and no kid-eating dogs had been released from secret cages. Stanley reached under his shirt, removing his USA Hospital Association-certified stethoscope, placing the listening end against the corner of a window. He looked at Robby, shook his head, then moved on to the next window, until they had gone around the entire house. There was nothing to hear, not even the sound of breathing.

"So we go upstairs, right?" Robby whispered. When Stanley nodded, Robby added, "How?" Stanley pointed toward the trampoline, which was still leaning against the side of the house. "You're going to jump up?" Robby asked. "Of course you are!" he said, slapping the side of his head. "It's obvious! The trampoline master tests his skill!"

For a moment Stanley saw himself as Robby must

be seeing him, bouncing on the tramp, higher and higher still, breaking all known height records. He imagined himself floating in the air, coming down as soft as a bird on the porch roof. He would have to remember to aim a bit sideways, of course. Stanley hadn't ever done that. Instead of landing on the roof, he might just jump into it. Or over it. Or miss it altogether. ESPN would just love to show *that*, he imagined. "Actually," he whispered to Robby, "I think it'd work better if I climbed up it instead. That's the plan. Come on, help me roll it over to the porch."

The porch attached to the house only a short distance from where the trampoline was leaning—it rolled easily and quietly into place. "You hold it steady," Stanley told Robby. "I'll use the frame and the springs to climb."

A moment later Stanley stepped onto the porch roof. He threw down the emergency rope ladder that Theresa had told him about, and Robby scrambled up, joining him. "Which window?" Robby whispered.

Stanley didn't know. He thought it was the first one, but he couldn't be sure. He hadn't watched that closely the time Theresa had escaped up the ladder. Still, she had to be in one of the rooms. Stanley placed his stethoscope against the first window; he heard soft breathing and nodded at Robby.

"Hold on a minute," Robby whispered. "Take off your mask. We don't want to give anyone a heart attack. See?" he said, smiling. "You're not the only one with a brain. Now go ahead, knock on the window."

The flutters in Stanley's stomach turned into waves. "What if it's not her window?" he hissed. "Ever think of that? All I heard was breathing—lots of people breathe, in case you don't know. What if it isn't Theresa?"

Robby just shrugged. "So we leave," he said. "Fast."

"What if whoever's in there doesn't want us to leave? What if they're big and fast and all they have to do is run down the stairs instead of climbing down that dumb ladder? Ever think of that?"

"Excellent!" Robby beamed. "And what if they start shooting? What if Theresa's parents aren't even her parents? What if they've been the kidnappers all along? That would sure explain a few things! Anyway," he said in a calmer voice, "we've been over this all before. I can't knock; I'm just the faithful companion. One hero per story—those are the rules. So go ahead, knock."

Stanley closed his eyes. He tried to imagine that this was only a movie, but his heart wouldn't stop pounding. For sure, he was no hero. Heroes didn't shake and get so scared that all they could think about was how badly they needed to use the bathroom. Besides, he'd never really expected to knock on Theresa's window—it was all just a game. Only he couldn't stop thinking about the way her mom had talked to her at the hospital and about how she was outside cutting the grass with a pair of scissors. What if she really did need help? *But how can I help?* Stanley thought. Then he thought, *But how can I not help?*

He knocked softly. When nothing happened, he knocked again. The drapes flickered open a crack. "Hi, Theresa," Stanley said, trying his best to smile.

"Stanley?" The drapes opened wider. Theresa slid the window up. "Stanley? What are you doing here?" She yawned sleepily, then suddenly came fully awake. "Stanley! If my parents ever catch you here, they'll kill me! You have to get out of here!"

"We're here to save you!" Robby said.

Theresa lifted the window fully open, leaning forward to see who else was on the roof. "This is my friend, Robby Lanorsky," Stanley said. "He's in Mr. Wright's class." Abruptly, he stopped speaking, staring at Theresa's face. With the drapes opened and the window up, light from the street flooded over her. Theresa had a black eye that went all the way around to her ear, and her other ear was swollen and red. There was a bandage on her nose too.

"Did you get into a car accident or something?" Robby frowned.

"I'm supposed to say that I fell down the stairs," she said. Her eyes went suddenly blank, not looking at Stanley, not looking at anything—but what was worse was her voice. Theresa's voice always sounded so full and lively, but now it was like the words were there but Theresa was missing. It was like listening to a recording. "I'm supposed to say that it was an accident, that it was my fault for being careless. I heal quickly, you know. That's what my mother always says. I heal quickly. Only I can't go to the hospital again. They keep records. If I go more than once, it gets reported. Mom gets reported." Theresa began to cry, sobbing without a sound, tears spilling down her cheeks, spotting her flannel pajamas.

Stanley couldn't speak. He had seen movies about it; someone had even come to their school and shown a slide show in the auditorium and answered questions. But he hadn't believed it. He didn't think parents really did stuff like that. Not real ones. "Your mom does that?" he managed.

Theresa nodded, still weeping. "She beats me up all the time," she finally said in a hoarse whisper, between sobs. "That's why we have to move so much."

"That's not right," Robby said. His voice was low

but not whispered; his face was so serious that he looked grown up. "That's just not right. Not at all."

Stanley tried to think of what to say, only nothing came to him. He tried to remember all the movies he had seen, what a real hero would do, only it didn't work. It wasn't because he was scared. For once he knew that wasn't the reason. It was because he really didn't know. "What should I do?" he finally asked. "I want to help, only I don't know how. Tell me what to do."

Theresa just stared at him, her eyes so dark and sad that Stanley felt tears coming to his own eyes. "You can't do anything," she finally said. Her voice was flat and lifeless again. "Nothing at all. Don't you see? This is where I live. That's all there is to it. This is where I live." Without another word, Theresa closed the window and pulled the drapes shut, disappearing.

Neither of the boys moved, and for a while neither of them spoke. Far away a car horn blared, but slowly, the sound of it faded, and the deep silence of night returned.

"Stan," Robby finally said, shaking his head, "what are we going to do?" And then again, "What are we going to do?"

what real heroes do

Stanley and Robby didn't talk much on the way back. They didn't try to hide or sneak about, either. Charles was still in his room with the door closed when they finally got home, so they each got an ice-cream bar from the freezer, then went and sat on the Lanorskys' porch, waiting. For what, they didn't know.

"Well?" Robby said after a few minutes.

"Well?" Stanley answered.

Robby shrugged, then nodded, as if they'd decided something. He took the last bite of his ice cream, toss-ing the stick into the bushes. "We tell my parents is what I'm thinking. I mean, we'll get into trouble for sure—but at least they'll know what to do."

They sat in silence for a moment longer. Then, without a word, Robby got up and went inside, returning with two new ice-cream bars. "Only they won't be home until nearly tomorrow," he added as he sat back down.

Stanley stared at the house across the street. His house. His parents would be up, watching TV. But they wouldn't be much help, he didn't think. Stanley scrunched up his face. Robby knew what his parents would do, so how come he didn't know about his own mom and dad?

"There's always my house," Stanley said, trying to make it sound casual

"Yep," Robby said, as if answering a question.

They sank back into silence, but now Stanley had the feeling that Robby was also staring across the street. At his house. Wondering. "I guess we might as well find out," he said at last. Stanley got up, walking down the front steps, head down, unwilling to think about what he was getting himself into.

The boys discovered Stanley's mom and dad sitting in their favorite opposite chairs, not talking, not watching the TV, but just waiting, as if they'd been expecting the boys. Which was exactly the truth.

"We got a very interesting phone call," his dad began.

"A *very* interesting phone call," his mom added.

"From Denver. You boys know anyone in Denver?"

Stanley and Robby looked at each other and shrugged, totally bewildered. Stanley tried to say something, but he couldn't figure out what it should be. Whatever he'd imagined happening, this wasn't it.

"Well, someone in Denver knows you," his dad said, looking more confused with each word. "And she told us the strangest thing. She said we might as well not go to sleep, because you two would be needing our help. Now, how on earth would she know that?"

"And how would she know that you've been out tonight?" Stanley's mom glanced at their grass-stained knees. "Which you obviously have. Which we will most certainly talk about later." Stanley could see that his mom was trying to look angry—only she wasn't. She kept blinking, as if she couldn't quite see straight. "But for now," she went on, "what I really need to know is this: How does that woman know Uncle Willie? She said she just met him tonight, that you introduced them. And that he's a very nice man. Willie Burns. That's how he introduced himself, she said. Willie Burns."

Stanley's mouth fell open. Denver, Uncle Alan, the list. He was beginning to understand. "Aunt Helen," he said.

"Right," his dad said. "Helen. Helen Karcher. And just to let you know why we haven't grounded you forever and"—he pointed to Robby— "called your parents . . . well, Helen asked us to not get angry with you . . . not, at least, until after we'd heard your story. Which was exceedingly strange," his dad said, looking more and more befuddled with each passing moment, "because she didn't know what your story would be, as it hadn't yet happened. But let me tell you this, buddy boy: She's on a plane out here as we speak, and she should be landing in . . ." Stanley's dad glanced at his watch. "Pretty soon. So whatever your story is, it had better be good enough to explain your being out when you should have been in, your being here when you should be there, and your being up when you should be asleep. And that, buddy boy, is a heck of a lot of explaining."

"Well . . ." Stanley hesitated, shuffling from foot to foot, wondering just how he'd gotten himself and Robby into this mess. And if there was any way out. "I know this girl in my class," he finally began. "And, well . . . her mother beats her up."

"It's not just a story," Robby added quickly. "We saw her. She had a black eye."

"And her face was all swollen."

"And her nose was broken."

"And she said that if anyone finds out, she's supposed to say she fell down the stairs, only that's not what happened, it was her mother."

"And not only that, but she says it happens all the time."

"I see," Stanley's dad said. He took in a deep breath. "And just exactly how did you find all of this out?"

Robby and Stanley both lowered their heads, glancing sideways at each other. "It was my idea," Stanley admitted. "When I was in the hospital, Theresa was there too, only she didn't see me, and I heard her mom say that next time it might be even worse. So when she wasn't in school this week, I was worried. So we called her. She didn't say it, but she needed help. And I thought—well, it's dumb, I know that now, it's really stupid, but I thought we could be heroes. So we went over to her house. We climbed up to her window. We were going to rescue her." He looked up at his parents. "She looked terrible, Dad. Really terrible. But the worst part was that she was crying and crying and saying how there was nothing anyone could do to help her." Stanley started crying then too. And then so did Robby. "It's not true that no one can help her, is it, Dad? Because it's not right, it's not right. Parents shouldn't do that, no matter what. They just shouldn't. We were going to rescue her, but we couldn't, we just couldn't, and we didn't know what to do."

Stanley's dad blew out a long breath, then slowly rose out of his chair, walking to the couch. He motioned to the boys to each take a seat beside him, and then, even more slowly, he put an arm around each of them, pulling them close. "I'm sorry you had to see a thing like that. You're right, it shouldn't happen. Not for any reason at all. And even though I don't ever again want you going out at night without telling us . . . you were brave. You were good friends."

"But what are we going to do?" Stanley blurted out. "It's not enough just to be good friends. We have to do something! We have to help her!"

"What are we going to do?" his dad repeated. "That's a very good question."

"At least Helen's phone call is beginning to make sense," Stanley's mom said. "I thought she might be crazy, she ran on so. I should have asked her more questions—it's just . . ." Stanley watched a strange, wonderful smile float across his mom's face. "I was so happy to hear about Willie. I mean, that he's Willie again."

"She told us an awful lot in a very short time," Stanley's dad said to his mom. "There wasn't much sense to it at the time. She was hurrying to catch a jet out here, though at the time I couldn't figure out why. Apparently, she'd always suspected her niece was being beaten, but she was never around to witness anything, because they always knew when she was coming. That's why she said that her niece needed protection but that there was nothing she could do, because she wasn't here. And she asked us to call the police, only when I asked her what about, she would only say that our son would tell us. So . . ." He shook his head, sighing deeply. "I might have to take tomorrow off." Then he reached for the phone, dialing 911. "Oh, heck, I'll definitely need tomorrow off. Stick around, buddy boy, the police will probably come here first, ask you some questions. Both of you. Then we'll probably all end up at . . . what's her name?"

"Theresa with an 'h,' Wasnicki with an 's,'" Stanley said automatically. Then, for the first time that evening, he smiled.

the beach

"Stanley!" his mom said. "What are you doing?"

Stanley looked up from his beach raft, which he'd managed to halfway stuff into the rear seat of the car. "It's my raft," he answered. "I always put it in the back."

"Well, not today," she chided. "Today your father's coming with us, or did you forget? I suppose you think he'll sit on top of the raft with you?"

Stanley hadn't thought about where his dad would sit; he almost never went to the beach with them. "Okay," he finally answered. "But he's sort of heavy. You don't think it will pop, do you?"

"Stanley!" his mom shouted.

"Lighten up," Jerry said to his mom. "He's only kidding you. I'll sit on the raft with the midget."

Their mom was about to say something else when their dad walked out. They all stared at him. Beneath his decade-old bathing suit, his legs were paper white. "Nice tan line," Jerry snickered.

Their dad looked down, then back up, a frown on his face. "Maybe you think I should just take off every Sunday. Become a beach bum, huh? I mean, what the hey-ho, I don't need to work! Come to think of it," he said, thoughtfully rubbing his chin, "that's not such a bad idea. I could put Jerry to work in my place. Saturdays, too—hey, this might save me a bundle."

"Hey!" Jerry said. "I didn't mean anything! Why do I have to go to work?"

"Lighten up," their mom said, tittering. "Your dad's only kidding you."

Just then a car screeched to a stop at the curb, gravel flying onto the sidewalk. Inside, Theresa and her aunt were both shrieking with laughter. "You're the worst driver I've ever known!" Aunt Helen sputtered, still laughing.

"Right!" Theresa said, also laughing. "It's better than the roller coaster!"

Uncle Willie got out of the driver's side door,

hurrying around to open the passenger door. "Ladies?" he said, helping them out. "And though it's not exactly the gentlemanly thing to do, I really must disagree. . . . Far from being the worst driver you have encountered, I am undoubtedly the best. It's just that I like to test my superb skills. Besides, we had to arrive in the nick of time—it's the only way to say good-bye! Reminds me of the time I was fleeing an irate Moroccan cab driver. . . . Ah, but that's a story for later."

"You're coming to the beach with us, aren't you?" Stanley asked, trying his best not to look at Theresa. He hadn't seen her in over a week—not since last Friday night at her bedroom window. She hadn't been in school since then, but she was safe, Stanley's parents had told him, staying with Aunt Helen at her hotel.

"Alas, no," Uncle Willie said. "I must take the fair ones to their appointed destinies, much as I've tried to tempt them into staying."

"That means he's driving us to the airport," Theresa explained. "We leave in an hour."

"Leave?" Stanley looked at the ground, blinking. "Where are you going?"

"Denver!" Theresa beamed. "I get to live with Aunt Helen. Isn't that totally great? The police said that if Aunt Helen didn't take me, I'd have to go into foster care, and besides, my parents didn't have a choice, anyway. Not with what you told them," she said to Stanley.

"Denver," Stanley repeated dully, hearing the word echo in his ears, just like in reading-aloud period. "I won't get to see you anymore."

"Of course you'll get to see me!" Theresa laughed. "You're my best friend!" She darted forward, and before he could duck away, she gave him a hug. "Aunt Helen says we can visit whenever we want. And I bought you a present." She handed Stanley a box. "Go ahead, open it!"

Stanley knew that his whole family was watching, but what did it matter? He was already beet red from the hug. He lifted the lid off the box and took out a cap, like the type he'd bought for his dad on Father's Day, only where that one had read BEST FATHER EVER, this one had printed on it BEST FRIEND EVER.

"The letters glow in the dark," Theresa said. She looked at the ground, smiling widely. Then suddenly, she looked up, right into Stanley's eyes. To his surprise, there were tears in her eyes. "Thanks," was all she said. "Just . . . thanks." Theresa hugged him again, then turned and ran back to Uncle Willie's car.

"Adieu!" Uncle Willie said as he closed the passenger's side door, hurrying around to the driver's side.

"Good-bye!" Theresa shouted as they sped off, gravel shooting out from the tires.

"Don't look so sad," Stanley's mom said to Stanley. "Your dad has some family in Denver; maybe we can go visit."

At that moment the Lanorskys pulled up in their car, Mr. Lanorsky tooting his horn. "Was that Willie? Nice to see him around again. You folks ready?"

Stanley's dad sighed, staring at the raft in the back-seat. "Ready as we'll ever be. Everyone in the car," Stanley's dad ordered. "Time is money, and we're wasting both of them!" Then, to Mr. Lanorsky, "We'll be right behind you."

Stanley didn't say much on the drive to the beach. He didn't know what to feel. He was happy that Theresa wouldn't have to live with her parents—only she wouldn't be in school on Monday. Or ever. And for sure, no one else was going to pass him notes. Or hug him. Stanley remembered how he'd shoved Steve Klemp out of the way that Friday afternoon. Well, maybe Steve Klemp would hug him. But it wasn't anything he was looking forward to.

It was a beautiful, late-summer day, and the beach was crowded by the time they got there. Once they had parked and hauled everything down to the beach, it was almost noon. Stanley's stomach began to rumble. At least he knew how to feel about that.

"I hope you made sandwiches without mustard," Robby said as they unpacked the coolers. "I'm not eating mustard. And no cucumbers, either. Cucumbers make me fart."

"Robby!" Mrs. Lanorsky said as she spread out a blanket. "Watch your mouth."

"What'd I say?" Robby asked, raising his hands questioningly. "Fart's not a cussword."

"Robby," Mr. Lanorsky said, "you're showing off. Please stop it."

Robby pouted for a moment, then grinned, motioning for Stanley to join him. He whispered something to Stanley, and after a moment of thinking, Stanley whispered back. "Yes!" Robby said. "Excuse me, Mom, Dad," he said, "for my use of such a vulgar word. What I meant to say was, I do not wish to subject our friends to a case of"—he looked directly at Stanley and smiled—"cucumber-induced flatulence!"

"Very funny, very funny," Mrs. Lanorsky said, tossing Robby a wrapped sandwich. Everyone else was laughing.

After sandwiches Jerry and Charles disappeared, walking up to the boardwalk to, as Jerry said, "check out the various moves." Robby and Stanley ran down to the water but almost immediately ran back.

"Too cold for you boys?" Mr. Lanorsky asked.

"Nah, the waves are too big," Robby answered.

"Too big for two dudes like you?" Mr. Lanorsky asked. "That's what they say nowadays, right? Dudes?"

Robby just looked at Stanley, rolling his eyes. "Sure, Dad. Sure."

"Stanley," his mom said, "find something else to do. I don't want you hanging around here all day."

"But, Mom," Stanley whined, "the waves are humongous, way over our heads." He turned to look at the waves again. "Send us out in those, and you'll have plenty more room in the car on the way back . . . if that's what you want," he added.

"Stanley—" his mom began, but Mr. Lanorsky interrupted.

"How about I go in with you? What about it, Robert?"

"Sure," Robby said.

For a few moments no one spoke. "Well," Stanley's dad finally said, stretching up from his blanket, "I suppose I could use a swim too, now that I think of it. Is that okay with you, buddy boy?" Stanley smiled widely, nodding. His dad peeled off the shirt he was wearing, revealing more paper white skin, and said, "Well, let's get moving!" He grabbed Stanley's hand and ran for the water, racing Robby and his dad.

"Whoa!" Mr. Lanorsky said as they got to the waterline. "Those really are big waves!" Stanley saw him winking at his dad. "Maybe it would be safer if you fellows rode on our shoulders."

"Yes!" Stanley and Robby shouted together.

Out in the water, feeling his dad gently rise and sink with each wave, Stanley felt as if he were back on the trampoline. He looked over at Robby and smiled. Then he looked down at the water, at his dad holding his legs. "Hey," he said excitedly, "I come from a hairy family too!" He leaned down so suddenly that he nearly toppled into the oncoming wave, but he managed to pull out one of his dad's chest hairs.

"Ow!" his dad said. But he was laughing.

Robby also leaned down, plucking a hair from his dad's chest.

"Ow!" Mr. Lanorsky said.

"Chest-hair wars!" Robby shouted, stabbing his fist into the air. "Whose is the longest?"

High above the waves, the boys leaned together, measuring. "Bad news, Dad," Robby said. "You lose. By a mile!"

Maybe not by a mile, Stanley thought, staring at the hair, *but by an inch, at least. Maybe more.* "Dad," he said solemnly, "I think we need to look into this."

"And why's that?" his dad asked.

"This could be a record." He examined the hair carefully, spreading it out fully.

Robby leaned over, examining the hair. "State record, for sure," he announced. "Maybe national. Maybe . . ." Stanley held his breath, waiting. "Possibly . . . Yes!" Robby finally announced. "World record!"

"Yes!" Stanley shouted, raising the hair high into the air. "Yet another world record for the Krakow family! Dad," he said eagerly, "turn around! Quick! Turn around!"

"Why?" his dad said, still laughing.

"The cameras, Dad! The cameras!" And so they all turned around, waving and laughing. And on the beach Mrs. Lanorsky and Stanley's mom aimed their cameras, clicking away.